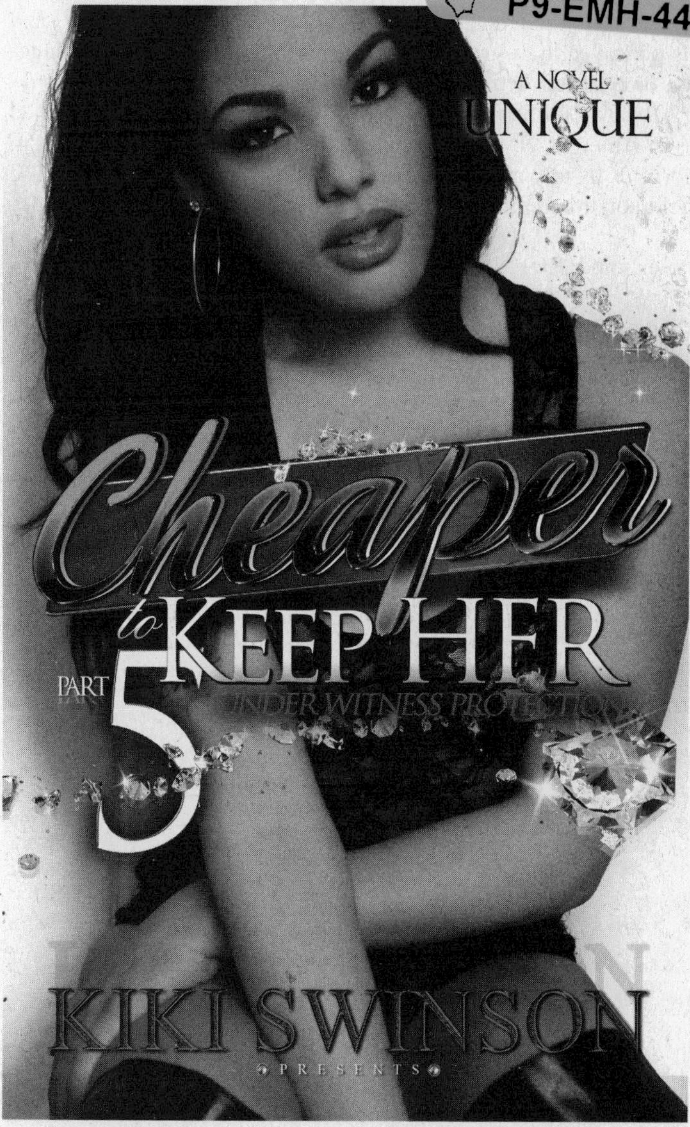

A NOVEL

UNIQUE

Cheaper to Keep Her

PART 5

UNDER WITNESS PROTECTION

KIKI SWINSON

PRESENTS

Publisher's address:

K.S. Publications
P.O. Box 68878
Virginia Beach, VA 23471

Website: www.kikiswinson.net
Email: KS.publications@yahoo.com

ISBN-13: 978-0985349547
ISBN-10: 0985349549

First Edition: May 2014

10 9 8 7 6 5 4 3 2 1

Editors: Letitia Carrington
Interior & Cover Design: Davida Baldwin (OddBalldsgn.com)
Cover Photo: Davida Baldwin

Printed in the United States of America

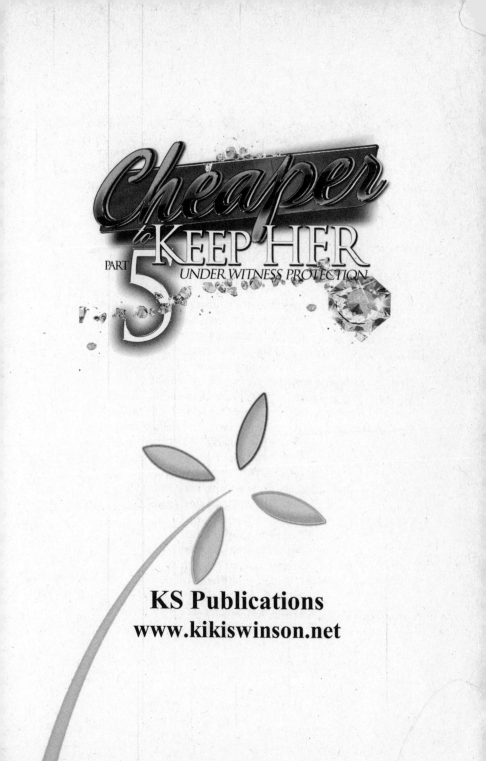

KS Publications
www.kikiswinson.net

Don't Miss Out On These Other Titles:

Wifey
I'm Still Wifey
Life After Wifey
Still Wifey Material
Wifey 4-Life
Wife Extraordinaire
Wife Extraordinaire Returns
The Candy Shop
Still Candy Shopping
A Sticky Situation
Sleeping with the Enemy (with Wahida Clark)
Heist (with De'nesha Diamond)
Life Styles of the Rich and Shameless (with Noire)
A Gangster and a Gentleman (with De'nesha Diamond)
Playing Dirty
Notorious
New York's Finest
Internationally Known (New York Finest 2)
I'm Forever New York's Finest (part 3)
Cheaper to Keep Her part 1
Cheaper to Keep Her part 2
Cheaper to Keep Her part 3
Cheaper to Keep Her part 4
Most Wanted (with Nikki Turner)
Green Eye Bandit part 1
Green Eye Bandit part 2
Ericka Kane part 1

Chapter One
WITNESS PROTECTION

"Which fucking way did she run?" I yelled. My voice boomed while I searched every inch of the backyard of the safe house.

"She climbed over the fence and ran north up the alley towards Cleveland Street." Agent Rome answered as he scrambled to get a grip on himself.

"How the hell did she get out of here? Was the alarm not working?" I continued to question Agent Rome while I made a dash towards the fence. Agent Rome followed my lead.

"I'm gonna take Wingate and see if I can cut her off there." I heard Agent Zachary's voice as she joined the chase.

"Keep your radio on," I yelled back at her.

"I will." she replied between breaths.

Agent Rome and I sprinted up the alleyway that led to Cleveland Street and made a quick right turn. I scanned the entire block with hopes of spotting Lynise's movements. But to no avail, she was nowhere in sight. I immediately panicked and spun around in a complete circle to catch my breath. "Where the fuck could she have gone?" I growled as I sat my sights on Agent Rome.

He stood there panting like he was out of breath. "Maybe she's heading towards the highway, hoping to get a ride to Norfolk." Agent Rome replied.

"That may be true, but for now we're gonna search this area thoroughly. My gut tells me that she's somewhere close by. So, go back to the house and round up all the agents except for Humphreys and tell them to get in their cars and comb every block within five miles of the house."

"Will do." Agent Rome said and then he scrambled back to the safe house.

I continued down Cleveland Street. The streets were pitch black, except for the dim lit streetlight at the corner of Cleveland and Monroe Street. So as I approached the streetlight, I saw a silhouette of a woman. My gun was already drawn. "Put your hands up and identify yourself." I demanded.

The moving object stopped. "Foster, don't shoot. It's me Zachary," she yelled.

"Show your face." I instructed.

"Okay. I'm coming in slowly." She replied.

I kept my pistol aimed, cocked and ready while I waited for Agent Zachary to reveal herself. After I confirmed her identity, I let out a long sigh and lowered my weapon. "Did you clear the area east of the safe house?" I asked her.

"Yes, I did,"

"And you didn't see her anywhere?"

"Nope. But I ran into a few junkies who said that they haven't seen anyone running around here fitting her description."

"That's bullshit. They saw her." I growled.

Agent Zachary gave me this, I told you so kind of look. "You just don't want to take the blame, huh?"

"What blame?" I replied. I knew where Zachary was going with this so I tried to play the dumb role.

"Foster, cut it out. You know you screwed up with this entire operation. Your little Miss witness fucked you, played you for a fool and now she's gone on her merry way."

"Zachary you have absolutely no idea what you are talking about. Lynise Carter is only a witness that I have been assigned to protect. That's it. And when we get her back in our custody, that's how things will resume. So let's not have this conversation again. Now are we clear on that?"

"Why are you getting so defensive?"

"Zachary you know I am not being defensive. I just want us to have a mutual understanding." I replied.

"Oh we have a mutual understanding, but it seems like every time your little girlfriend throws a little fit you always make special provisions for her."

"Mann what's your position?" I continued to probe everyone's location.

"I'm in the car circling the entire neighborhood." He replied.

"Well Mann, stay on patrol until I say otherwise. Rome I want you to meet me back at the house. It's time to go to plan B."

"What about Zachary? You do know she's out here too." Rome questioned me.

"Zachary is with me. And we're headed back to the house now."

"Roger that," Rome spoke back through the radio and then all communication went dead.

Going into search mode!

Chapter Two
My Worst Fucking Nightmare

I knew Agent Foster and the rest of those fake cop ass FBI agents were pounding the streets looking for me. But I took off running as soon as I hopped over the fence on Agent Rome's pussy ass. I couldn't believe how that chump ass nigga played me. I mean this nigga literally tried to take me out. He must've forgot I was from the streets. I was not about to let him eliminate me. No way.

I had walked at least two miles before my feet started feeling it, which is why I flagged down a cab. I was on Jefferson Avenue walking by a gas station when I saw a cab driver pumping gas into his car. I approached him and asked him if he'd give me a lift. "You got money?" he asked me.

"Yeah, I got money." I assured him.

The cab driver ended up talking my head off during the course of the drive to Norfolk. "What's your name?" he wanted to know.

"Pam," I lied.

"How old are you Pam?"

"Twenty-five." I lied once more.

"Got a boyfriend?"

"Yeah. And he's crazy jealous too."

"What do you think he'll do if he sees me and you talking?"

"He'll be mad and take out his pistol."

"Does he do that every time he sees another man talking to you?"

"Yep." I replied in an unenthused manner. I figured if I'd answer his questions nonchalantly than he'd leave me alone. But that didn't happen in this case.

And as soon as we crossed over the bridge and traveled through the Hampton Bridge Tunnel, I noticed that he took the first exit, which was the Willoughby Spit exit. "Why are we taking this exit?" I inquired.

The cab driver looked back at me through the rearview mirror and said, "Shut up bitch! You're about to go on the ride of your life."

Fear stricken all over again, I managed to cry out, "Oh my God! You're that serial killer that's been killing all those women."

"Yes I am pretty girl! And you're gonna be my next slave."

I couldn't believe that I was face to face with the serial killer that had been raping and killing all those innocent women. And what was really fucked up was that this nigga drove a cab, so women fell right into his lap. But I wasn't going to let this nigga get the best of me. I was a fighter and I was from the hood. Allowing him to do what he did to those other women wasn't in the cards as far as I could see it. In other words, I wasn't going down without a fight.

I reached for the door to bust my way out of the car but the door wouldn't open. I tried to unlock the door but that didn't work either. I panicked. "Open this fucking door right now!" I screamed.

By this time the cab driver had pulled over to the side of the road. I looked around and noticed that the street we were on was deserted. There was only one streetlight lit on the entire fucking block. The shit looked spooky. And to know that I was in the company of a fucking serial killer only made things worse. This guy was a straggly looking old black guy who had to be in his late forties. His facial hair and the hair on his head looked rough and unmanaged. From the back seat, this man looked like he was every bit of 160 lbs, if not more. I could also tell that he didn't have much height to him. After sizing him up I psyched myself into believing that I could take him down.

"Let me out of this fucking car!" I continued to scream while kicking on both the window and the door.

"Bitch if you break that window I'm going to kill you!" his voice boomed.

"Fuck you! You better let me out of this motherfucking car now!" I screamed as loud as I could. I had to let this bastard know that I wasn't afraid of him.

While I made it blatantly obvious that I wasn't going down without a fight, he in turn showed me that he was ready to go toe to toe with me. Out of nowhere this fucking maniac produced a Taser gun. I saw a spark and then two wires with hooks at the end of them followed. And before I even realized it, fifty thousand volts of electricity hit my body. I tried to fight it but the movement in my body started slipping away from me. And then it stopped.

Had death finally claimed my life?

Chapter Three

THE MANHUNT

Once we realized that Lynise wasn't in the immediate area, all of the agents met me back at the safe house. I ordered everyone in the house to meet me in the downstairs meeting room. "As we all know, our witness has escaped. What we don't know is her whereabouts. With that said, we're gonna have to gear up and start a full blown manhunt until she is back in our custody."

"Have you contacted anyone back at headquarters?" Agent Rome asked.

"No I haven't." I replied.

"Well, don't you think you should?" Rome's questions continued.

"As the senior Officer at this safe house I am in charge of everyone here so that gives me the discretion to make those types of calls. So, to answer your question, no I don't think I should call headquarters. I will handle this matter on my own."

"What if we don't find her?" Agent Zachary asked.

"Let's be a little more optimistic Zachary."

"Foster she's right. What if we don't find her?" Agent Mann chimed in.

I was starting to get a little aggravated by all of my agents' questions. They noticed it too. "Listen carefully guys, because I am only going to say this once. Our federal witness has fled on foot so we're gonna have to gather up all of our resources so we can find her and bring her back into our custody. Now if for some unfortunate reason we can't find her, then we will call headquarters. In the meantime, keep you eyes and ears open and make sure everyone's back is covered. We can't have another casualty like we just had when we were escorting our witness back from the police precinct. We have to be in control of everything around us. We cannot afford to ever have that done to us again. Understood!"

"Yes sir," everyone said in unison.

"Does anyone have any questions to address before we leave out of here?"

"Do you plan to leave an agent here just in case she comes back?" Agent Zachary asked.

"I'm glad you asked, because you were the person I had in mind."

"Me?!" Agent Zachary replied. I could tell in her voice that she was surprised by my gesture.

"Yes, you."

"But what if she doesn't come back?" Agent Zachary tried to reason. She wasn't at all happy with me.

Whether she knew it or not, it wouldn't be a good look to have her with me anyway. She was indeed a good agent, but sometimes she'd make a lot of her decisions based on emotions. And right now, the last thing I needed was emotions. I needed to find my witness and I refused to let Agent Zachary blow our cover.

Now before I could assign additional work details Agent Rome chuckled and mumbled, "With that large bounty on her head we oughta' just let her go. I mean, she'll probably be dead within 24 hours anyway."

"Would you mind repeating that agent?" I spoke up. His words were jumbled up so I didn't hear what Agent Rome said.

"Listen boss, all I'm saying is that why don't we leave her be. We got popped pretty bad transporting her from that interrogation she had with those local cops the other day. I mean, come on, why risk one of our own? She left here because he didn't want to be here." Rome explained.

"No Rome, she left because someone screwed up. And for the life of me I'm trying to figure who that was?"

"What are you saying?" Agent Zachary blurted out. She seemed curious as to where I was going with this.

"I'm saying that someone in here either dropped the ball or they let her go freely and tried to make it look like she escaped on her own." I explained. I scanned every agent's face with every word I uttered from my mouth.

"So, you're trying to say someone here let her go?" Agent Rome responded defensively.

"Yes, I am. But if you have another explanation, then I'm all ears." I replied with certainty.

"No disrespect, but I think you're out of your damn mind. What agent on this work detail would jeopardize their career over letting a witness go? That's insane."

"Well, if you think I'm insane then tell me why you were the only one outside when she escaped? And how is it that she was able to get out of the house without the alarm going off?" I asked Rome. I needed some fucking answers and I needed them now.

"I can't tell you how she got out of the house without the alarm going off. But I do know that you don't give her enough credit." Agent Rome started off. "She's not a walking target for nothing. Even the local homicide detectives want a piece of her ass. They knew she was lying to them when they interrogated her. And if you continue to act like she's a fucking angel instead of the criminal that she is, then we're going at this thing wrong."

I chuckled at Agent Rome's remark. "How do you suggest we should go at it?" I asked. I was very curious to hear what else this idiot had to say. Something wasn't quite right with Agent Rome and I intended on finding out what it was.

"I think we should count our losses and head back up north." Rome added.

"I agree." Agent Zachary said.

"I don't care who agrees with who around here. The fact still remains that she was placed in our custody. She is the only person alive that can help us put Bishop away for life. Does it even bother you that he murdered our commander Joyce? Knowing that he took her life should be more of a reason for you to want to go out there and find our witness. We could use Lynise in so many ways."

"Yeah, he's right you guys. We gotta' get her back." Agent Humphreys agreed.

"Where do you want us to start looking?" Agent Mann chimed in.

"She's from Norfolk. So, I think that's where we need to set our sights on." I suggested as I walked over to the closet near the entryway of the kitchen. In the closet contained a briefcase with most of Lynise's personal information stored inside. After I grabbed the contents of it from the briefcase, I xeroxed copies of the last three addresses where she resided and I also made copies of addresses of people she knew. We could not leave no stone unturned. And once we were equipped with the information we needed I assigned work details and then we carried on with our mission.

"Can I talk to you alone before you leave?" Agent Zachary asked me.

"Sure," I told her. I instructed Agent Humphreys to wait for me in the car and then I followed Zachary to the kitchen. "What's up?" I asked her.

"I just wanted to say I'm sorry for taking Agent Rome's side."

"You don't have to apologize to me for that. You're entitled to have your own opinion. So, I'm good."

"You're not mad are you?"

"Look Zachary, are we finished here?" I spat. I was becoming annoyed by all of her questions. Time was ticking rapidly and I needed to get out of there.

Thankfully she got the hint and told me she was done talking. After I got into the car I looked back at the safe house and saw Zachary looking through the mini blinds of the living room window. I knew she was upset with me, but with her thick skin she'd get over it. *Women are so fucking emotional!*

Chapter Four

WHERE AM I?

My entire body ached when I regained consciousness. And when I realized where I was I wanted to yell for help, but I couldn't. A salty tasting cloth that looked like it was torn from an old sheet was tied around my mouth. Even the smell of it became unbearable. But what really shattered my heart was when I saw the wretched and sordid conditions my kidnapper put me in. I was strapped down in an old ass wheel chair placed directly beside a filthy sofa chair. A couple of the springs from the sofa stuck out through the cushions. It was a sight for sore eyes. The carpet was severely worn out. The walls were covered in old wooden panel. There was also a huge clutter of relatives' pictures nailed to the wooden panel. The lampshades had the old school fringes hanging from it.

The house wasn't that big. I could see the kitchen from where I was sitting. The refrigerator was an old green color. The kitchen table set was even old and out dated. The stove was on its last leg too. Every piece of furniture and ceiling fixture in this place looked like it had been purchased back when Kennedy was President. Picture a house from a fucking horror movie, well that is what this place reminded me of.

"Honey, she's awake." I heard an older lady say with a heavy southern draw. Her voice came from the entry-way of the TV room so I turned to see who this voice belonged to. To my surprise, the elderly woman was white. Now if my memory serves me correctly the cab driver that drug me to this horror scene was black. So, why is this 5'1, frail, old lady here? She can't be down with this kidnapping shit. I mean, for God sakes, she doesn't look like she could harm a fly.

Seconds later, I heard footsteps scurrying across the floor behind me and then the cab driver appeared before me. He smiled at me as he began to pull my hair back away from my face. The old white lady stood next to him. She looked like she was taking inventory or something. "Isn't she beautiful mama?" he asked.

"Yeah, she looks better than those last two you brought here. What's her name?" She replied.

"Pam."

"Stop fucking touching me!" I belted out. But since I was gagged my words were jumbled up.

"Sounds like she's trying to say something." I heard her say.

"She's probably saying she loves me mama." The guy commented as he continued to touch my hair. He was giddy to say the least.

"Are you fucking people crazy? I didn't say I loved him." I screamed. But once again these psycho ass people weren't hearing my words. I mean, did he really believe that I uttered the word loved? Was he out of his fucking mind? And why the hell is she standing here with this crazy ass man like everything is peachy? And what does she mean the last two girls? Am I not leaving out of this motherfucking place alive?

"Where did you get her from?"

"I picked her up in Newport News."

"Well, she's probably hungry." The old lady said.

"Yeah, you're right mama. Her face does look like she's famished." The fucking cab driver replied.

"I don't want none of y'all fucking food! I want y'all to let me go." I screamed once more. This time tears began to fall from my eyes. I was becoming so overwhelmed with these people. I was literally about to have a nervous breakdown.

"Oh mama, why do you think she's crying?" the guy asked. He looked somewhat concerned. Seeing me cry made it seem like he was having seconds thoughts about kidnapping me.

"I don't know child. Maybe she misses her mama."

"Are you missing your mama?" the guy asked.

I nodded my head, letting him know that that wasn't it.

"Then what is it?" he pressed the issue.

"I want you to let me go." I screamed even though I knew they wouldn't understand me.

Thankfully he loosened the gag from my mouth. It hung around the chin area of my face. I felt some kind of relief. "Listen to me. I am not hungry. And I don't miss my mama. I want to go home." I pleaded with them while I continued to cry.

"But why do you want to go home?" he wondered aloud.

"Because I miss my family and they're gonna wanna know where I'm at." I lied.

"But what about me? What about my feelings?" he questioned me.

"I'm not trying to hurt your feelings. I mean, we can still see each other." I continued to conjure up lies.

"No. I don't believe you. You're gonna leave me just like all the others." He snapped. His whole demeanor changed. He went from a nice guy to an abusive weirdo in the blink of an eye.

"I promise I won't leave you." I tried to convince him.

"No. Shut up! You're a liar just like all of those other girls." He screamed and then he abruptly yanked on the gag and forced it back around my mouth.

After he made the gag tighter he stormed off into another part of the house. His mother continued to stand there before me. "You think you're too good for my son, don't cha'?" she gritted her teeth.

I shook my head.

"Well, you're acting like it missy. But let me tell you something. My boy is special. He's a good boy.

And I won't let anybody else hurt him. You understand me?" She yelled and then she smacked me cross my face as hard as she could. I swear I saw stars. My vision became blurry as I watched her leave the room. When I was able to hone back in on my surroundings I was alone once again.

I could not believe how I got myself into yet another deadly situation. First, I was running from Duke Carrington. But after I had him ambushed and done away with, the Carter Brothers put a bounty on my head. And once I turned on Bishop he got in on the action to get rid of me too. Now I'm here at this looney ass people's house. How bad can my life get? Do I have a death wish? Or is it Karma? Whatever it is, I've got to get a handle on it before I end up like Diamond and Bishop's sister.

According to the clock on the wall in the TV room, the serial killer and his crazy ass mama left me in the room for almost two hours. It had been a total of nine hours since I escaped the safe house. I was starving and I had to pee badly. I battled with the decision about whether or not I should tell those crazy ass people that I had to use the bathroom. My gut feelings told me that that wouldn't be a good idea. The way these people were bugging out, they'd want to accompany me in the bathroom while I took a piss. Having either one of them watch me pee gave me an eerie feeling. I knew then that I needed to try to hold my urine as long as possible.

Twenty more minutes had passed before I heard movements from those fucking weirdos. The serial killer appeared first. He smiled at me like he was happy to see me. Did he just not leave out of here like he wanted to kill me? I wasn't a doctor but something told me that this crazy ass nigga was bipolar.

"Hi there beautiful. I miss you." He said as he approached me.

I wanted to vomit in my mouth after he told me he missed me. Nigga you were in the next room. And you just saw me not even two hours ago. Get your act together and let me go.

"Are you hungry? Can I get you anything? he asked me after taking the gag from my mouth.

"I just want to go home." I began to cry, tears falling from my eyes.

"What are you talking about? You're already home." He replied.

"No I am not. This is not my home. Please let me go." I cried harder.

"I'm sorry. But I can't do that. You are my soul mate. We're going to be together forever."

"No we are not. You don't even know me."

"Yes I do. And you are the one for me."

"Stop saying that. I am not the one for you. I am not your soul mate. So just get that through your head."

Saying nothing about my comments, he grabbed me

by my throat and began to choke me. He was squeezing the breath out of me and I was growing weaker and weaker. "So you are not my soul mate, huh?"

I tried to answer him, but I couldn't get a word out. I had to figure out how I was going to get this man to stop choking the life out of me.

"I'm sorry. Yes we are soul mates." I uttered. My words were barely audible. But thank God he heard me.

At that moment, he loosened his grip from around my neck. I felt kind of relieved, even though the pain around my neck was excruciating. I coughed for about three consecutive minutes.

"Aaaahhhh, are you okay?" He asked me while he massaged my neck. This guy was fucking nuts.

I tried to speak between coughs but I couldn't. So I nodded my head.

What I really wanted to do was tell this guy to get his fucking hands away from me. I mean, how can you try to kill me with your bare hands one minute and then try to console me the next minute? This guy was definitely off his rocker.

"What's going on in here?" His mother blurted out as she entered back in the TV room.

"Oh I was just standing here asking my wife to be, if she was hungry?"

"For Christ's sake Jimmy, it's ten o'clock in the morning. Of course she's hungry," she continued.

"Well what do we get her?" Jimmy wanted to know.

"Give her some of that oatmeal in there." His mother suggested.

"But what if she doesn't eat it." Jimmy said.

She slapped him across his shoulder. "Boy, don't question me. Just do what I say." She instructed him.

Jimmy scrambled out of the TV room after his psycho ass mother demanded that he get me a bowl of oatmeal. "You're gonna love my oatmeal. I've been making it for Jimmy since he was very young." She told me.

"Who cares?!" I said underneath my breath.

"Did you sass me young lady?" his mother asked me. She leaned over in my face like she wanted to smack me again.

"No ma'am." I replied, still feeling the throbbing pain around my neck.

"You better not. Because me and my boy will not stand for anyone else disrespecting us. Do you understand?"

"Yes, ma'am."

"Good."

"I need to use the bathroom." I managed to say. I couldn't hold it any longer.

"Jimmy come on back in here and take this girl to the bathroom." The lady yelled.

"No. Don't call him. I would rather have you to take me."

"Oh no. I'm an old lady. I'm not strong enough to push you in that wheelchair.

"I'm not that heavy." I tried to convince her.

"You look heavy to me." She replied. She was adamant about not taking me to the bathroom, which was a load of crap because she smacked the hell out of me earlier. So to stand here and act like she's too weak to push me to the bathroom is pure bullshit!

Jimmy entered back into the room with a bowl of oatmeal with a spoon inside of it. "She's gotta use the bathroom?" he asked.

"Yeah. And she tried to get me to take her. But I told her I wasn't pushing her heavy butt. She won't throw my back out."

"Yeah mama, I don't want you doing anything." Jimmy sat the bowl of oatmeal down on the coffee table a few feet away from me. Then he took the locks off the wheels and began to push me in the direction of the hallway. The bathroom was only a few feet from the TV room. So as he pushed me down the hall, the wood floor started cracking like they wanted to give way at that moment. I held my breath a few times hoping that I wouldn't fall through the floor.

When Jimmy stopped the wheelchair in front of the bathroom he untied my hands and feet. Boy what a relief that was. "Now I'm gonna let you go in there by yourself, but you better not do anything stupid." He told me.

"I won't." I said as I got up from the chair.

Once inside the bathroom, I didn't turn on the light because it was fully lit by the sun shining through a very small window with bars sealing it from any intruders from the outside. The bathroom itself was filthy. There was no tile left on the floor. It was completely chipped away. There were several rotten boards coming up from the floor. It brought in a major wind draft from underneath the house. The boards were very weak so I walked around it.

Before I sat down on the toilet I looked at the seat cover and then I looked down inside the rusty toilet bowl. The sight of it was revolting. It made me sick to my stomach. I couldn't imagine how long this damn thing hadn't been cleaned. "Look now, are you gonna pee or what? 'Cause I ain't got all day." Jimmy said. He stood there with the bathroom door slightly ajar like he planned to watch my every move.

"Are you going to stand there while I pee?" I got up the nerve to ask him.

Jimmy cracked a smile. "Don't tell me you're scared to pee in front of me?"

"No I am not scared. I just need a little privacy."

"What do you need privacy for? We're not going to hide things from one another. We're going to be together forever," he continued to explain. But I wasn't trying to hear that. I wanted to use the bathroom without being watched so he needed to get it through his head sooner than later. Before I gave him a rebuttal I knew I couldn't be sarcastic. This guy needed to be handled differently. I knew I had to handle him with kid gloves in order to get what I needed. So I took a deep breath and said, "Listen Jimmy I know you and I are soul mates. And I know that we're going to be together, but there are some things that women have to have and one of those things is privacy. All I'm trying to do is use the bathroom and freshen up so I can look good for you while I'm eating breakfast. That's it. So are you going to give me that?" I asked, trying to act like he was in control. Reverse psychology was a very needed tactic at this moment.

After Jimmy thought for a few seconds, he ended up giving me the green light to use the bathroom alone. "I'm gonna let you use the bathroom by yourself but remember what I said. No funny business."

"Trust me, I won't." I convinced him.

Once the bathroom door was shut I exhaled. I felt a sense of freedom even though I was locked up in these people's house. All kinds of thoughts rushed through my head. It was hard to think straight. The bottom line was that I needed to figure out a way to get out of this fucking place. And in order to do that, I needed to win his trust.

Winning Jimmy’s trust will be easy. But getting his mother’s trust was going to be very hard. I could tell that she wasn’t feeling me from the start. And when it came to her son, she’d be even more aggressive to shut things down. So I figured that if I got Jimmy to side with me, maybe I’d be able to draw a wedge between them and ultimately gain my freedom. It was a game worth playing.

It took me longer than usual to pee. I had to squat over the toilet seat to prevent my ass from touching it, which in turn caused me to pee around the toilet seat and on the floor. What was even worse about this situation was that these people didn't even have toilet paper so I could wipe my ass. To prevent Jimmy from having an excuse to come into the bathroom, I tried to shake as much urine off of me and then I pulled my panties and my pants back up. I didn't bother to flush the toilet because it didn't look like it worked. I did what most niggas do, shake it off and keep it moving. "I'm done." I said to Jimmy, who was waiting outside the bathroom door.

"He opened the door. Are you ready?" He asked.

"Yes." I replied and took a seat back in the wheelchair.

He wheeled me back into the TV room and fed me the oatmeal after he tied my wrists and ankles back up.

I've got to get away from these inbred motherfuckers!

Chapter Five
I Got a Bad Feeling

It was my call to go out and do a full scale search for Lynise. I could give a dozen different reasons why she needed to be found. One being that my ass was on the line would be the first one. The second reason was that I had developed feelings for her and if I was unable to find her before those other goons got to her, then I'd be fucked up for life. Figuring out how she got away still bothered me too. I knew Agent Rome wasn't being straight with me. I'd bet money he had something to do with her leaving the safe house. And if that were the case, then it would soon come out.

Agent Humphreys and I drove in one car while Agents Rome and Mann road in the car behind us. I was glad that Humphreys and I were alone because I had some questions for him. "You've worked with Rome before, right?"

"Yeah."

"What do you know about him?"

"Well all I know is that he just got transferred to our office a little over a year ago. And Agent Joyce paired him up with Agent Mann not too long after that."

"Do you think he's trustworthy?"

"I hadn't heard anything bad about him."

"Well I think he had something to do with Lynise getting away."

"What do you think happened?"

"I can't exactly say what happened. But I do know that he had something to do with the alarm system. Lynise didn't know how to disarm it. So there's no doubt in my mind that Rome was behind it. And besides that, how is it that he was the only one that knew Lynise was escaping? Why didn't he let one of us know that he was outside?"

Agent Humphreys thought for a moment and then he said, "It's kind of hard for me to point fingers at Rome, but when I think back to what he said about her running away, he made me a little suspicious."

"Yeah, he's hiding something and I'm going to find out what it is." I assured him.

"I would too. But while you're doing that just tread lightly because Agent Rome holds a lot of weight within the bureau."

"I don't care what he holds." I snapped. "If he had anything to do with her escaping then he will get dealt with." I continued. I had to make Humphreys know that Lynise was a high priority witness. So, if he in anyway tampered with our operation then there's going to be a price to pay.

Lynise initially worked as a bartender at a strip club called Magic City so that was where we began our search. If there were information to get, then that would be a great place to start. Unfortunately, the club wasn't there. I noticed a big pile of debris where the club used to sit. Humphreys and I got out of the vehicle to get a closer look. After our assessment, we realized that the place had been burned down. "Was it burned down?" Agent Rome asked from the driver's seat of his car.

"Yep. That's exactly what happened." I told him.

"Well where do you want to go next?" he asked me.

"Let's take a ride through a couple of housing projects and see if we can get lucky. Who knows, maybe we can find someone who'd give us an idea of where she could be."

"I personally don't think that would be a good idea." Humphreys pointed out. "If you want to ride around those neighborhoods then that's one thing. But I don't think looking for people to give us information would be a wise thing to do."

"Okay well, let's just ride around the areas where her profile has listed as places she most frequents."

"Cool." Humphreys agreed.

****

By the time three o'clock in the morning rolled around, the agents and I decided to head back to the safe house after we scoured the streets of every housing project of Norfolk and Virginia Beach. When we walked through the doors Agent Zachary greeted us. "Well, did you find her?" she asked me.

"No."

"Where exactly did you guys go?"

"We searched all of the bad neighborhoods in Norfolk and Virginia Beach."

"Did you stop by the strip club where she was a bartender?"

"That place is no longer there."

"What do you mean it's not there?"

"It was burned down."

"Well what about the other strip clubs in that area? Did you stop by any of them?"

"We stopped by a couple of them. But we got no action."

"So what's next? Are you guys going to do another full search tomorrow?"

"Yeah. We're gonna have to do something. And we're gonn have to do it fast."

"Think it would be a good idea if you reach out to some of her family? Because when I looked into her file I noticed that she had a couple of cousins that lived in Norfolk."

"Yes. But I want that to be the last resort."

"Why?"

"Because I don't want to alarm anyone. And I don't want to let the wrong person know that she is somewhere in the area." I replied while I took off my jacket.

"Well yeah, that makes sense." She said.

"Well, since I'm gonna have a long day tomorrow, I'm gonna go ahead and turn in so I can get some sleep."

"Me too." Humphreys said.

I noticed Agent Rome and Agent Mann followed suit while Agent Zachary stayed in the living room area of the house.

Immediately after I got into bed I realized that my body wouldn't allow me to sleep. I tossed and turned all night thinking about how I was going to handle things going forward. I meant what I said when I made the comment about reaching out to Lynise's family being my last resort. At this very moment, at least a dozen people were looking for Lynise so if I wanted to get her back into our custody safely, then that meant that I'd have to take all the necessary precautions. My circle of agents was small and I liked it that way. You can keep drama to a minimum when you work with a small group of people. The only problem I had with my circle was Agent Rome. He just doesn't carry himself as a trust-worthy guy; especially with all of the lame ass excuses he gave me when I questioned him about him and Lynise in the backyard alone. Nothing he said added up to me. So, I planned to keep a close watch on him and his partner Mann, just in case I needed to handle things with them a little differently. You can never be too careful with this world we live in. It would either be me or them.

I choose me.

Chapter Six
These Motherfuckers Are Crazy

It's been two days since I've been in this hellhole with these fucking fruitcakes, which has enabled me to figure out Jimmy's schedule. He drives his cab at nights. And during the day he's either sleeping or worrying me the fuck to death. There was not a minute that went by that he didn't express how much his sick ass loves me. On top of that, he brought his mother and I each a dozen of red roses when he walked in the house this morning. "Got you and my mama some beautiful roses." He smiled.

His mother smiled too. But I wasn't in the mood to smile. I was tied down to a fucking wheelchair twenty-four hours a day, wearing the same clothes and hadn't washed my ass, my face or brushed my teeth. So, I say fuck the roses and give me a one-way trip ticket out of this joint. I'd be happy once that happens.

Jimmy handed his mother her dozen of roses first.

After she took them she admired how nice they were and then she thanked him. Instead of placing the roses in my hands, Jimmy set them on my lap since my hands were tied. "Do you like 'em?" He asked me.

"Yes. They're really pretty." I lied. I could care less about these fucking roses.

"I just got them from this guy down there by the pier."

"I hope you didn't spend a fortune on them." His mother said.

"Oh no. I got a great deal for 'em."

"Put mine in some water." His mother instructed him.

Jimmy took them from her hands. "Want me to put yours in some water to?" He turned and asked me.

"Yeah. That's fine."

Jimmy took both my roses and his mother's to the kitchen and stuck them into two different vases with water filled half way. He brought them back to the TV room and sat them down on the coffee table so that we could see them.

I watched him through my peripheral vision as he smiled at the roses. He admired them like they were huge achievements. "You did good son." His mother commented.

"Thank you mama. Thank you." He responded.

Jimmy stared at the roses for at least another sixty seconds. When he finally looked away it was because his mother was excusing herself from the room. "Well I guess I can go in my room now that you're home." She said as she stood up from the old ran down couch.

Jimmy stood up. "Mama, why are you leaving so fast?"

"Because I am tired. I've been sitting in this chair all night long watching this girl for you. So now it's time for me to go and lay down in my own bed."

"Do you need any help?" Jimmy seemed concerned.

"No. I'm fine. "She said and slapped him on his arm like he was irritating her.

"Do you want me to bring you some hot tea to your room?"

"No. I've drank enough tea this morning for ten people."

"Okay. Well, let me know if you need me." He told her.

After his mother waddled down the hallway to her room I heard her close her bedroom door. It was like music to my ears. And I figured this would be a perfect time to start working on Jimmy. He needed to be broken down slowly. I knew I was dealing with a whack job so if I screwed up, then I could forget leaving this place alive. Jimmy turned around and looked at me. "I guess it's just me and you now."

I gave him a fake ass smile.

"Did mama feed you breakfast?"

"No. I told her I wanted to wait for you to cook my breakfast." I replied seductively. I had to turn the charm on very thick.

This made Jimmy smile. "Oh really!? I like the sound of that. So what do you want to eat? He asked.

"I would love to have some eggs if you have 'em."

"Well let me go and see." He replied and skipped off into the kitchen.

I heard the refrigerator door open. He waited a couple of seconds to speak. "Doesn't look like we got eggs. But we got milk and a box of corn flakes."

"What kind of milk is it?" I asked. I really didn't care about the type of milk that was in the refrigerator. My goal was to make conversation with him so he could feel comfortable talking to me. Being able to talk to me freely would begin to make him trust me.

"We only drink one percent milk around here." He said but then he paused. "Oh shoot, it's expired," he continued.

"It's okay," I told him.

I was indeed hungry. But cereal and milk definitely would have not done the job for me. I preferred not to eat anything else from this house. I hoped I'd be able to talk him into going back out to get me something to eat. If it worked, then I'd know for sure that his defenses could be broken.

"Hold up a minute, I found some pancake mix. And we got a half bottle of syrup." He said cheerfully. Boy did he pop my balloon. But I couldn't let him get me while I was down. I came back and pretended to be allergic to syrup. "I can't eat syrup," I lied.

He rushed back into the TV room holding both the

box of pancake mix and a bottle of syrup. "Why not?" he asked. He looked so disappointed. But I wasn't fazed by it. I was fighting for my life whether he realized it. So, if it took me to shake up his emotions, then so the fuck what!

"I'm allergic," I finally said, giving him the most sincere expression I could muster up.

"Ahh man, really." he replied.

"Yep,"

"Well, I guess I'm gonna have to think of something else to fix you."

"What about getting me a steak biscuit from McDonald's?" I suggested.

"But, I can't leave you in the house while mom is resting."

"She won't know." I tried to assure him.

"Oh no. Mama would kill me if she came out here and found out that I left you in here by yourself." He explained. And what was so bizarre about his explanation was that he went straight into child mode. I mean, he sounded just like a fucking nine-year-old kid. His mannerism and everything had taken me aback.

"Are you okay?" I asked him. At this very moment, he did not act like the man that kidnapped me against my will 48-hours ago.

"Yes. Of course I'm okay." He said, shaking the child-like disposition off. It was like he snapped out of it just like that.

"Are you sure you're okay?" I pressed the issue.

"Yeah. I'm good." He replied. He gave me the impression that he was trying to get a handle on his emotions. I didn't know whether to pry a little more or leave well enough alone. This fucking guy was unstable so I knew that the best thing for me to do was tread lightly.

"You know what? You're right. We don't want to upset your mama by you leaving me here alone. So, let's think of something else to feed me." I added. I had to make him believe that he was right and that he was still in control.

"Okay. Yeah. Let's do that." He agreed.

He headed back into the kitchen and ended up making me several small pancakes. And instead of pouring syrup on top of them I told him to leave them plain. Under normal circumstances I would've eaten a steak biscuit from McDonald's. Agent Foster would've had one of his flunkies around the safe house run out and fetch me the whole breakfast meal. I can't tell you how badly I wished I had not left that house. I never thought I'd say this, but I sure missed Agent Foster.

While this nut case fed me the pancakes, I began to pull out little intimate details about himself. I needed to know who I was really dealing with. "How old are you?" I started off saying.

"How old do I look?" he asked me and then he smiled. He was acting like we were playing a fucking guessing game. I wasn't trying to get to know him so we could be a couple. I just wanted to know if he had all his fucking marbles. But I allowed the chips to fall where they may and went along with his bullshit.

"You look like you're thirty-five."

"Nah, I'm forty-seven." He smiled once more.

"I hate to pry, but is that your real mother in the other room?"

"No she's not. But she's had me since I was five years old."

"Did she adopt you?" I continued to question him.

"Yeah. She was my foster mother at first. And then after my fifth birthday she decided to keep me."

"Do you know what happened to your real mother?"

"No."

"Do you wish to know?"

"All I need is that lady in the other room. She took me when no one else would. So I owe her my life."

"Do you take medication?" I asked. I swear I didn't mean for that question to come out of my mouth.

He looked at me like I was crazy. I braced myself for what would happen next.

"No. I don't take pills." He answered me. He didn't seem upset by my question. "But mama does give me vitamins and stuff."

"What kind of vitamins?" I probed.

"Just some vitamin C and iron pills."

"Oh, okay. That's good." I replied, trying to downplay the conversation. I didn't want him to blow my spot up by telling his mama I gave him the third degree. She was an old lady but she had more sense than I gave her credit for.

Mr. Psycho and I continued to chat about things that really didn't matter to me. So I had to continue reminding myself that by my doing this would eventually win his trust and garner my freedom.

Now I wasn't naïve by a long shot. I knew that I would have a fight on my hands the day I managed to leave here. They're going to go for blood but I will be up for the challenge, especially since my life will be on the line. I also needed to take into account that I may have to take their lives before I escape. As many dead bodies that I've seen, killing may become natural.

In my life there is never a dull moment.

Chapter Seven

THE MANHUNT CONTINUES

I was reluctant to let Agent Zachary ride with me to do another search for Lynise, but I decided to do it anyway. Agent Humphreys stayed back at the safe house while Agents Rome and Mann followed in a separate car.

"Thank you for letting me ride with you today." Zachary said.

"You don't have to thank me." I told her.

"I know I don't. But with everything that's going on, I appreciate you giving me the chance to make things right between you and I."

"It's no problem." I commented and then I switched the topic of our conversation. "Wanna do some face to face investigating today?" I asked her. I needed to get a few people on board to help us find Lynise. See Agent Zachary was a woman, and the good thing about her was that she didn't look like an agent. She'd be perfect to go undercover."

"I'll do whatever you need me to do." She told me.

Getting her to execute my plan meant we were one step away from perhaps finding Lynise. I thanked her for it. "Thank you." I said.

"No need for that. That's what I am here for." She told me. I wanted to believe that she was being sincere but I couldn't. Zachary was full of shit. She hated Lynise because she knew I fucked her and she knew that I had feelings for her. She'd railroad Lynise and hang her out to dry if she had her way. So, anything that remotely sounded like she had Lynise's best interest at heart was pure bullshit!

It was 11 o'clock in the morning when we arrived in Norfolk. It was my idea to check out a few of the strip clubs. Club Diamonds was the first stop. Rome and I parked our cars at a Chinese restaurant directly across the street from the club. I instructed Zachary to go into the club and act like she was looking for a job. She was gamed for it. Before she exited the vehicle she removed her government issued firearm and badge from her hip and left it on the car seat. "Just act natural." I told her.

"I got this," she said and walked from the car.

While I watched Zachary as she walked towards the club, I noticed a couple of drug dealers standing next to their cars in the parking lot. Both guys were black. One was flashier than the other. The one that was less flashy had a few words for Zachary. I couldn't hear what he was saying, but from the looks of his facial expression, I could tell that he was flirting with her. Zachary ignored him and continued on into the club. After the door closed behind her, I looked down at my watch to keep count of the time.

"Do you guys have visuals?" I radioed to Rome and Mann.

"Yes, we've got visuals." Agent Rome radioed back.

"Stay on guard." I instructed him.

"Roger that," he replied.

I watched the front door of the strip club from the time Agent Zachary walked inside until the time she came out. It took her a total of fifteen minutes to go inside and come out. The two guys that were once in the parking lot had left. A black, G-63 Mercedes Benz truck pulled up while Zachary exited the club. The truck stopped and then the window rolled down. "Do you guys see what I see?" I talked into the radio.

"Yes, we're locked in on the black SUV." Agent Rome answered.

"Can you see inside?" I asked.

"No. The tint is too dark." Rome replied.

"Neither can I. So, let's just hang back and wait on her cue." I told him.

"Ten four," Rome said and then cut off communication.

I couldn't see the driver but my guess was that it was a man. My heart rate picked up while I watched Agent Zachary's body movement. She looked in my direction a couple of times. But she did it in a way to prevent the driver from looking my way.

After a few more words were exchanged, I saw a man's hand pass her a business card. She smiled at him and then she walked away from the truck. I radioed Agents Rome and Mann. "She's on the move," I said.

"We got a visual." Rome replied.

"Be on guard fellows, because whoever is driving that vehicle hasn't exited it yet. So, my guess is that she's being watched."

"Roger that." Rome added.

As Agent Zachary crossed the street she looked directly at me. So, I motioned for her to walk by my car and continue on into the restaurant. I had no idea who was in that SUV. But whoever it was took every precaution to conceal their identity. Thankfully, Agent Rome and I had parked our cars behind other patrons' cars that were dining at the restaurant. If not, then our cover would've been blown.

After waiting for close to thirty minutes, the driver finally exited the SUV. He was a black male. He was tall in stature and he looked to be in his early forties. He was dressed casually. To sum it up, he definitely looked like new money.

Immediately after he went into the club, I called Zachary and told her to get her ass out of the restaurant. Seconds later, she scrambled to my car with a take out container. Once she was inside the car, I pressed down on the accelerator and fled the scene. Agent Rome followed.

"You will not believe who I was just talking to?" she started off saying.

"Who?" I said. I wasn't in the mood to play a guessing game. I wanted to get to the facts.

"I just met the Carter brothers' cousin Malik." She said. Hearing her utter the words Carter brothers was like music to my ears. How ironic was that? Was it fate that brought us here?

"You have got to be kidding, right?" I smiled. I was becoming anxious. It was like she wasn't coming out with the information fast enough. "Was he alone?" I wanted to know.

"Yes."

"Did he tell you why he was at the club? He is the owner?"

Zachary pulled his business card from her front pants pocket. "That's what his card says." She replied as she handed him the card.

I took a look at the business card. And there it was printed in black ink, Malik Carter, owner and operator of the Club Diamonds. I got a chilling feeling looking at the card so I handed it back to Zachary. "How do you know that he's the cousin?"

"Because he told me. He asked me if I ever heard of his two older cousins who own most of the businesses and strip clubs in the area?"

"What did you say?"

"I told him that I hadn't. So, he comes back and says that I must not be from around here because everybody knows the Carter brothers."

"What did you tell him?"

"I told him I had just moved here from Philly and that I was looking for work. So, he wanted to know if I was a dancer. I told him no. But I did tell him that I wanted to be a waitress. And that's when he gave me his card and told me to call him later."

"Great job Zachary! Great job." I commented.

I gathered all the agents together when we got back to the safe house. I gave Agent Zachary the floor so she could bring all the agents up to speed about her chat with the Carter brothers' cousin Malik. After she filled them in on the details I stepped in and told them how we were going to put Zachary to work on the inside so she could gather all the Intel we needed. I had a hunch that Lynise was in the area. And hopefully by doing this, this would bring us closer to finding her.

Later that night, I picked up a throwaway phone from a nearby convenient store and got Agent Zachary to call this Malik character. We needed to get the ball rolling. When he answered his phone, Zachary put him on speaker. "Hi is this Malik?"

"Yes it is," we all heard him say.

"Hi Malik, this is Priscilla." She lied. Priscilla was

the name she had given him when she met him earlier in the parking lot of the strip club.

"It's good to hear your voice." He told her.

"Likewise."

"So you want a job, huh?"

"Yes. Are you going to hire me?"

"How badly do you want to work?" he pressed the issue.

"Well, I told you that I just moved to the area and that I was living at a relative's house. So, the quicker I get a job the better situated I can be."

"When can you start working?"

"I can start tomorrow."

"Of course you can. Just meet me at the club tomorrow night and we'll talk about the specifics."

"Okay. Well I guess I'll see you then." She told him and ended their call.

The minute after Agent Zachary hung up with the strip club owner, we put a plan in motion. "Listen you guys, Agent Zachary is going to be our eyes and ears while she's waitressing at Club Diamonds. Every night one of us will go in the club and act as patrons so we can make sure that she's not in harms way." I began to explain.

"Have you thought about how she is going to get there? You know she can't drive one of our undercover vehicles." Agent Humphreys pointed out.

"I made a call back to the office and they're getting things in motion so we can pick up a vehicle in this area by tomorrow." I explained.

"What about some new clothes?" Zachary asked me.

"I put in a request for that too. But while we're waiting for that to be approved, I'm gonna let you use the credit card I was issued for this trip."

"Are we gonna still continue on search missions while Zachary is working at the club?" Agent Mann wanted to know.

"Yes, we will still continue on with our search." I assured him. "Any other questions?" I asked, looking around at all the agents standing in a huddle.

"When you called headquarters, did you tell them that our witness had escaped?" Agent Rome asked.

"No, I didn’t." I replied.

"Well, how did you explain you needing a car and an approval to buy a new wardrobe?" his questions continued.

I knew Rome was trying to fuck with me, but I let his bullshit roll off my back. "When you’re the head of command you don't have to answer certain questions.

"So are you going to eventually tell them?"

"Yes I will. And when I do, I'm gonna inform them that you were the cause of her escaping."

"What the fuck you mean by that?" Agent Rome roared. The veins near his temple nearly exploded.

"It is, what it is Rome? You and I both know that you had something to do with our witness escaping."

"That's bullshit! I'm not going to let you stick that one on me."

"I'm sorry, but it's already done. You did what you did, and that's final."

Agent Rome felt the heat falling down around him. So when it became unbearable, he charged at me. Luckily, Agents Mann and Humphreys stopped him in his tracks. "I'm not gonna let you play me like I'm some kind of punk. And I'm not going to take the fall because you failed to do your job properly."

"Technically my job is to oversee you and the rest of the agents in this house. And while I was overseeing, I noticed that you were doing God knows what with my witness in the back yard of the house while it was pitch black. And up to this very moment, you still have not come up with a good enough reason why that happened."

"I told you what happen. Now if you don't believe me, then it's on you." He commented sarcastically.

"Come on you guys, we gotta' break this up. We got a job to do and we won't be able to do it if we're at each others necks," Agent Humphreys said.

Agent Rome and I retreated to opposite sides of the safe house. Agent Zachary accompanied me while Agent Rome sat downstairs with the rest of the agents. This separation did wonders for us.

I still looked at him like the snake he was.

Chapter Eight
I Need to Get Out of Here

"Jimmy, aren't you supposed to be at work?" The old white lady asked after she entered into the TV room. It was a few minutes after midnight.

"I'm off tonight mama." He replied his eyes glued to the television, while I was still strapped down to the same fucking wheelchair like I was disabled. Jimmy's goofy looking ass was sitting on the love seat only a few feet away from me.

We watched all the news stations around the clock. It was his mother's idea to stay informed. I'd eavesdropped on a couple of their conversations. It puzzled her to know that there hadn't been any missing persons reports on me. I knew it would blow their minds if they knew that I was under witness protection. And when you were under witness protection, every agent assigned to your case had to stay tight-lipped when it came to the witnesses.

"Has she been giving you any trouble?" she asked as she sat down on the other sofa.

"Oh no mama, she's been really good. That's why I didn't put the gag back around her mouth." He replied, refusing to take his eyes away from the TV.

"What's happening on the news? Anything new?" she continued to question him.

"Nah, nothing new. They just keep talking about the last two girls I killed."

"Have they found their bodies yet?" she seemed interested, like they were playing some fucking hide and seek game.

"Nope. But they will if they keep searching Bay View Drive near the Ocean View beach."

"Okay, but don't forget that you dumped their bodies out there over two weeks ago and it's crab season. So when they do finally find them their faces won't be recognizable because those blue crabs are going to disfigure them."

"Yeah mama, you're right. I didn't think about that." I heard him say. I was in total awe as I listened to these two talk about two innocent women's lives. They acted like two coldhearted axe maniacs. I have never seen anything like this before, even when I hung out in the hood. Niggas I knew that took someone else's life didn't sit around and talk about it like it was all fun and games. They killed the person and kept it moving. That's it.

"Any word on her?" she asked as she pointed in my direction.

"No mama. Nothing."

"That's strange," she commented.

I laughed to myself without even realizing it. Only for that moment, it felt like I had one up on them, even though I was being held against my will. I knew all along why they were watching all the news channels like a hawk. So, for them to wonder about what was going on in my life that prevented my name from being plastered all over the TV made me feel like there was some hope for me.

"Hey girl, where are you really from?"

"I'm from Newport News." I lied.

She gritted at me. "Are you lying to me?"

"No ma'am." I lied once again.

"Well why ain't nobody reported you missing?"

"I don't know."

"Oh you know."

"I swear I don't."

"Mama, I believe she's telling the truth."

"Oh shut up! You don't know what you're talking about. She could've been lying and you wouldn't even know it." The lady snapped.

"But mama, I already told you where I picked her up from."

"Picking her up from Newport News doesn't mean

that's where she lived. She's 's a whore Jimmy. And whores travel from place to place."

"I am not a whore." I blurted out. This bitch really offended me. She doesn't know shit about me. And if I weren't strapped to this chair, I would close her mouth permanently. It didn't matter that she was old. Old bitches can get smacked too.

"Mama she is not a whore. She's a good girl." Jimmy tried to defend me.

"What time did you pick her up the other night?"

"Around this time."

"Well there you go. Only whores hang out on the streets this time of night."

"I was only on the streets that time of night because my car broke down." I lied. I had to think of something, even if it was a lie to prove to her that I wasn't a ho.

"I don't believe that for one minute."

"Mama, can you please be nice to her?" Jimmy pouted like a child.

"I will be nice to her after she tells us the truth."

"But what if she's already telling us the truth?"

"Oh Jimmy get the stick out of your ass. I can see that this girl doesn't have an ounce of honesty in her body from a mile away. She is just like all the other girls you brought home."

"Mama, no she's not. She's special." Jimmy defended me once again. This time he got up from the chair and immediately embraced me. The feeling of his touch made my skin crawl. But I couldn't show the emotions because his mother was watching my every move.

"Mama she's different from the rest of them." Jimmy continued and then he kissed me on my forehead. Right then and there, I wanted to jump out of my skin. His kiss was wet and it felt disgusting. But I held onto my composure. I had to. I had to prove that everything this lady was saying about me was wrong. It was hard to do. But I was making it work.

"Oh bologna!" She replied and then she blew us off with a hand gesture.

Thankfully Jimmy didn't hold me in his arms too long. After he diffused the conversation about me, he let me go and headed back to his seat.

Everything became quiet for the next ten minutes that is until one of the local news stations reported an Amber Alert, which is a child abduction. Every one of us tuned into the broadcast. The report lasted about a minute and a half. And when it was over, the old lady had something to say. "I betcha' the mama's boyfriend had something to do with that little girl being kidnapped."

"It would be a shame if that were true." Jimmy added.

"Yeah, it sure would. I just don't understand why grown ups won't pick on someone their size. Leave the children alone. Their innocent."

"So, you're against adults abducting kids?" I blurted out. I couldn't hold my words back. I had to put this old bitch in the hot seat.

"Oh absolutely." She replied confidently.

"Well, why is it okay for your son to kidnap innocent women? I mean, women are an unfair advantage if you put them next to a man. Am I right?" I continued. This bitch was making me go there with her ass.

"Are you getting smart with me young lady?" she snapped.

"No. I just wanna know why isn't it okay to kidnap a kid but it's okay to kidnap a woman?"

Jimmy's mother stood to her feet and started walking towards me. Jimmy jumped to his feet too and stood between his mother and I. That didn't stop her from spitting fire at my ass. She released the fury. "Don't you ever question me again about what is right and what's wrong." She spat, as she waved her fingers at me. "Women have done my son wrong for years. They played on his feelings. And they used him for as long as I can remember. So sure, it's okay for him to do anything he wants to do to women. They deserve everything that comes their way because they are manipulative, greedy, spiteful, and they don't care about anyone but themselves."

"I'm not like that. I'm a good person." I choked up. I became upset listening to this fucking lady tell me how women were. But I wasn't like that. When I worked back at the strip club as the bartender, life back then was good to me. I worked and I minded my business. I also had a best friend that ended up turning against me because of a heartless ass nigga. Now the both of them are dead. And the nigga who killed them wants me dead. So again, I was a good person until my world fell down around me. The person I am now is only trying to stay alive long enough to maybe draw social security one of these days. That is it.

"Oh get out of here with those meaningless tears." She commented and then she turned back around and sat in her seat.

Jimmy leaned over towards me and wiped the teardrops from my face with the back of his hands. He seemed bothered by my tears. "Mama, you made her upset."

"She ain't crying for real. She's putting on an act." She replied sarcastically.

Unbeknownst to either of them, I was crying because of where my life's choices had taken me. I was ready for a change. But this wasn't the change I had hoped for.

Jimmy's dumb ass finally got his mother to settle down. They rambled on for at least another twenty minutes. But nothing they said even made sense. I drifted off to sleep a couple of times, but they always seemed to find a way to break my sleep.

"Mama, you know I love you right?"

"Yes, baby. I know you do."

"And you know I'll never stop loving you, right?"

She chuckled. "Of course I know that, silly."

"Well, would you stop giving Pam a hard time? I know you don't trust her. But something in my heart is telling me that she's the one. So, just give her a chance."

The old lady paused for a second and then she said, "I'll tell you what. I'll back off of her until I see different. But you gotta' promise me that you'll never let her come between what you and I have. Do you understand?"

"Yes, mama. I understand." I heard him say and then their chat ended.

I sat there in that fucking wheelchair wearing three-day-old clothes and had not bathed once. So, to hear this fool act like he and I were going to live happily ever after was a fucking joke to me. I'd rather kill myself first before I lay down and fuck this pervert. This fucking grease ball and his mother are going to be in for a rude awakening.

Reality is about to set in.

Chapter Nine
TREADING ON THIN ICE

Agent Zachary and I went to the mall to purchase a few clothing items so she could start the waitress job at Club Diamonds tonight. We headed to Patrick Henry Mall, which was the nearest mall from the safe house. We shopped at a few stores and came out with a few sexy form fitting blouses and dark colored tights. Once she felt she had enough things to go undercover, we headed back to the safe house. On the way there Agent Zachary wanted to talk about ways to smoothly navigate through her undercover work tonight. I could sense that she was extremely nervous. "You know you're gonna be fine, right?"

"Yes."

"So why the long face?"

"Have you thought about who's going to accompany me tonight?"

"I'm gonna be with you tonight so I can feel the place out."

"Are you gonna be there the entire night?"

"No. I'm gonna go in a few minutes before you get

there. And then when you get off I'll be watching your back from a block away. That way I can follow you back to the safe house."

"Thank you. I appreciate you making sure that I'm okay."

"That's what I am here for." I told her.

"Do you think we're gonna find Lynise through this channel? Because remember, there is a huge bounty on her head. So if it were me, I wouldn't hang out at a strip club owned by a close relative of the men who want me dead."

"I totally agree with you. But look at it this way, even if Lynise may never show her face at that club, there could still be some buzz going around about where she is. I just want you to keep your eyes and ears open. That's it."

"How do you want me to handle that Malik guy, because you know he's gonna be making passes at me. You heard him in action when I put him on speaker yesterday."

"Just try to keep it clean. Let him know that you have boundaries and that he needs to respect you."

"What if that doesn't work?"

"It will work. Women always have the power. But most of you give up so easily, because you got to have a man."

Zachary chuckled. "You are so right. And now that I think about it, I know a lot of women who do it."

"If y'all would just stand your ground, you'd have

the world eating out of your hands."

"I wish it were that easy."

"It can be." I assured her.

Back at the safe house I laid down a couple of rules before we headed out. The main concern I had was for her to understand that her safety came first. "Don't try to be tough." I instructed her. "And don't try to be a hero. You aren't there for that. Someone will always be around to step in if something goes south. So, just relax and get as much information you can until I pull you off this detail." I continued.

"What if I see someone dealing drugs? Am I supposed to turn my head?"

"First of all, we're out of our jurisdiction. So of course, I want you to turn your head. We are only here to find Lynise. Anything outside of that does not concern us." I replied.

"What if someone gets killed?"

"Now that's different. But again, let's try to keep your involvement in the club to a minimum. We don't have a lot of time left to find our witness, so let's stay focused. The quicker we can get intel, the quicker we can get out of there."

"Okay. I think I can manage that."

"Good. So, let's get started."

Club Diamonds was packed from wall to wall with

drug dealing thugs. From the outside the club looked cheesy. On the inside the décor was suitable for the mixed crowd that was spending money tonight. There were a few white men. But there were more black men siting around the stage. I even noticed a couple of black women throwing single dollar bills at the exotic dancers. In all there was five, big, black bouncers in the club. Two stood at the front door, one stood near the bar area while the other two stood on the opposite ends of the stage. They were definitely in position to do damage control if need be.

While I checked out my surroundings and the dancers of course, Agent Zachary came strolling into the club. Our eyes met but then they soon departed as she turned her attention to the woman standing behind the bar. I couldn't make out what was being said, but after the bartender got the attention of the bouncer standing next to the bar, I figured out that she needed to be escorted to another part of the club. They both disappeared behind the stage. I sat there patiently with a Corona in hand and waited to see what would happen next. Five minutes passed and there was no sign of Zachary. Then ten minutes passed and there was still no Zachary. But after waiting a couple more minutes Agent Zachary finally reappeared with the bouncer walking behind her. I let out a sigh of relief that all was well.

I allowed her to get in the groove of things before I asked her to come and take a drink order from me. I wanted to make sure we didn't look suspicious talking to each other. "I got worried when you went behind the stage with the bouncer." I told her.

"He had to take me to the back office to see Malik."

"So, he's here?"

"Yes, he's here."

"That's shocking because I didn't see his SUV outside."

"He's probably driving something else."

"So, what did he say?"

"Nothing but that he's glad to see me. And that he wants me to come back and see him before I leave for the night."

"Was he alone?"

"Yeah, he's alone. He was on a call when the bouncer and I walked into his office."

"Well, you be careful."

"I will." She said. But before she walked off she said, "Let me get you something else to drink so we don't stick out like sore thumbs."

I smiled. "Yeah, why don't you do that."

Just like I had planned, I left the strip club and hung out in my car until Zachary ended her shift. I waited in my car for almost three hours before Zachary walked out the front door. It was two-thirty in the morning to be exact. And she wasn't alone. A short Hispanic looking woman walked alongside Zachary but then they parted ways. The woman got into a white Range Rover sport. She beeped her horn at Zachary as she drove out of the parking lot. Zachary got into the Toyota Camry our department head approved for her. I waited a few minutes before I followed her back to the safe house. I had to make sure she wasn't being followed. And when I realized that she wasn't, I followed suit.

Agent Zachary arrived back at the safe house before I did. When I walked into the house she was sitting in the kitchen telling Agent Humphreys how her night went. "For it to be a Thursday night, I raked in one hundred and thirty-two dollars in tips."

"That's awesome." He told her.

"Tell me about it."

"I see you like your new job." I interjected.

She smiled. "It wasn't half bad." She replied.

"Did you get a chance to talk to your boss again?" I questioned her.

"No. As a matter of fact, he got a call and left the club in a rush."

"Did anyone say why he left in such a rush?"

"No. No one said anything about it. Everybody pretty much mind their own business."

"Well who was that woman you walked out the club with?"

"Her name is Camille. She's one of the other waitresses at the club."

"Did she tell you how long she's been working there?"

"Yeah, she said she's been there almost six months now."

"Did she say anything negative about the club?"

"All she said was for me to watch out for the other women in the club because they are shady."

"That's it?"

"Yep. That's it."

"Well, I'm sure there's more to her story. So, just keep your eyes and ears open. And good job on your first day."

"I will. And thank you." She said.

I sat back and watched Zachary exit the kitchen. I could tell how important I made her feel when I acknowledged that she had done a good job. Agent Humphreys noticed it too. "Everyone knows that she has a sweet spot for you." He commented.

"Is it that obvious?" I asked.

"Come on buddy. Everyone in this house knows about her feelings for you. She will do anything you ask her to do. No questions asked." Agent Humphreys continued.

"I know." I said and then I paused.

"Don't get quiet now." Humphreys joked. "The damage is done."

I sighed heavily. "Don't remind me." I finally said. It was exhausting thinking about how I fucked up and slept with Agent Zachary. Agent Humphreys was right, Zachary was only sticking her neck out because of her feelings for me.

"So, how do you think this undercover work is going?" he changed the subject.

"So far so good."

"Have you thought about how long we're gonna work that detail?"

"I'm thinking maybe a couple weeks." I replied. But I wasn't too sure. I honestly didn't know how long we were going to work the strip club detail. At this moment, I was desperate to try anything to find Lynise.

"Have you decided when you're going to call headquarters to let them know about what is going on?" Humphreys probed.

"Yeah, I figured if we didn't find Lynise in the next couple of days, then I would let them know. That way we can get more agents to join forces with us."

"Foster you know I'm going to always have your back. But I think that you're going about this thing wrong. We should've called headquarters immediately after our witness escaped."

Agent Humphreys poked holes at my decision not to report Lynise's escape to headquarters. All egos aside, I had to admit that Humphreys was right. I should've reported the incident to our acting-director. But I felt it was necessary for me not to because Joyce who was the head of our department was just murdered. It was blatantly obvious that we have a mole in our department. I just needed to find out who it was before I gave them that sensitive information. I was not about to let no one breach my operation. After Lynise is found, we will move her to another secured location and move forward with our investigation to lock Bishop's drug dealing and murdering ass up.

I swear I can't wait to see that day.

Chapter Ten

WHO'S REALLY IN CHARGE?

"Would you please let me wash up? I've been sitting in this wheelchair for four days now. I know y'all have smelled me by now." I complained. It was nine thirty in the morning and I was falling deeper into depression. The foul smell coming from my body was becoming unbearable.

"My mama doesn't think it's a good idea to leave you in the bathroom."

"But you leave me in the bathroom to piss!" I snapped. I had become disgusted with these people.

"I know. But it's gonna take you more time to bathe. And she's afraid that you may try to escape." He tried to whisper.

"Escape and go where? I will be naked for God's sake." I reasoned.

"I understand that you're upset. But you're gonna have to calm down before she comes in here."

"I'm tired of calming down. I need you to stand up for me." I said. I knew this would be a great time to try to get into Jimmy's head. His mother had a stronghold on him. She controlled everything about him. So, while she was in her bedroom with the door closed I decided to try to chip away at some of the damage she had done to him. But before I could open my mouth she walked into the room. My plans were crushed. She looked directly at me. "Do you have something to say to me?" she asked.

I choked up. I wanted to say something but my mouth wouldn't move. I wasn't scared or anything. I guess I was a bit surprised that she heard me talking to her lunatic of a son. I braced myself because I knew her wrath was about to be unleashed.

"I just want to wash my ass!" I yelled.

Within a blink of an eye, this bitch lunged back and swung at me. "Don't you ever talk to me like that again!" she roared.

Luckily for me, Jimmy stopped her from hitting me. "Well, let me wash up," I yelled back. I wasn't backing off from this damn lady. I needed to put her in her place. She and her son had violated me enough.

"I'm not letting you do a damn thing. Now sit in that seat and shut up before I make you regret the day you were born missy." Her voice sounded demonic now.

"My name ain't Missy. It's Lynise," I replied, seeming irritated. But my reaction to all this madness didn't matter. What mattered was that I had just told these two nut jobs what my real name was. I was caught red handed. Jimmy's facial expression turned from concern to shock. Everything seemed to happen in slow motion after he turned his attention towards me. His mother stood beside him and watched him as he became enraged. "So, your name isn't Pam? It's Lynise," he said, gritting his teeth.

"No, Pam is my middle name." I managed to say. I knew I had to keep this lie going. But it didn't work. Jimmy grabbed my neck and began to squeeze the breath out of me. I coughed while gasping for air. "You fucking lied to me!" He snapped. "My mother was right. You are just like those other girls. I fucking hate you!"

"Son, I told you she was not to be trusted. I told you." She chimed in.

Jimmy continued to hold a death grip around my neck as the pressure from his hand seemed to take life from me by the second. I could see death in his eyes as his mother applauded his efforts to kill me. It was apparent that she wanted me dead more so than he did. She got her rocks off seeing me plead for my life. This bitch was more sinister than the devil himself. It can't get any worse than that.

After Jimmy crippled me for what seemed like a lifetime, I noticed that I was slipping out of consciousness. And all I could think about was that I was going to end up like his last two victims. The difference between them and I was that I had no one looking for me, but U.S. Marshalls and federal agents.

When it felt like I was about to take my last breath, Jimmy released his hand from my neck. I was still coughing. "What are you doing? Kill her!" I heard his mother yell as I dropped my head low.

Please wake me up from this nightmare!

Chapter Eleven

SNAKES IN THE GRASS

I assigned Agent Humphreys to accompany Agent Zachary on her third day at the strip club. While they were gone I decided to take the other car and ride around a bit. I took Lynise's file with me just in case I needed it. Time was of the essence and it was running out.

I drove around the city of Virginia Beach. But I concentrated on the neighborhoods that were documented in her file. My agents and I had already searched this area but I felt there were a few rocks that still hadn't been turned over.

After scouring the urban neighborhoods of Virginia Beach, I threw in the towel and headed back to the safe house. It was close to 10 p.m., so I stopped by a Chinese spot about two miles from the safe house. I ordered vegetable fried rice, paid the Asian woman behind the counter, and when she handed me my food, I thanked her and left.

Upon my return to the safe house I found nothing out of the ordinary except that Agents Rome and Mann weren't downstairs in the meeting room watching TV, which was were they generally hung out.

Once I sat my food down on the kitchen table I went to look for them to let them know that I had come back. I went upstairs to the second floor. And when I reached the top step I heard voices coming from the bedroom that Agent Mann was assigned to when we first got here. One of the voices was Agent Mann's and the other voice was Agent Rome's. I heard some laughter but then I heard Lynise's name come up. So, instead of letting them know that I had come back, I tiptoed as close as I could to the bedroom door to ear what was being said. "Foster is really in over his head with this operation." I heard Agent Rome say.

"I told you we need to call headquarters and let them know what's going on." Agent Mann said.

"You know we can't go over his head. The acting director would crucify our asses if we did that." Agent Rome added.

"Not if we tell them that there's a bounty on her head." Agent Mann said.

"You may have a point there. But remember the least amount of agents we have looking for her the harder it'll be to find her. And the longer she's on the streets the more likely someone will see her and take her ass out. And when that happens, she'll never be able to blow our cover." Agent Rome pointed out.

"Yeah, you're right. And we can't have that."

"No. We can't have that." I heard Rome sigh.

"So what are we going to do moving forward?"

"We'll just continue to act like we're looking for her. And who knows, maybe one day soon we'll see on the news that someone has collected on her bounty."

Agent Mann found humor in what Rome said and burst into laughter.

I on the other hand, I didn't find any of that bullshit they said funny. I mean, how the hell are you going to go against the grain? We're supposed to have one another's back especially in this field of work. So, to hear this joker telling his partner that they're going against me was fucked up. And what could Lynise know about those fucking creeps? What could be so damaging that they wanted to feed her ass to the dogs? Whatever it is, I am going to find out about it. But until then, I'm going to hold my composure and act like I never heard any of this shit. Knowing that these motherfuckers were snakes made me look at them totally different. They honestly could not be trusted, which brings me to the decision that I was going to have to tell someone about this. But who? Was I going to be able to trust Agent Zachary with this information? Or would it be in my best interest to only tell Agent Humphreys? Whoever I decided to tell was going to have to keep this secret close to their hearts or we would all be screwed.

Keep your enemies close!

Chapter Twelve

FUEL TO THE FIRE

After Jimmy almost choked the life out of me, he stormed off in another part of the house. His mother sat in the chair across from me and made a bunch of snide remarks after I fully regained consciousness. My neck was so sore it was hard to swallow the saliva in my mouth. "My son is gonna listen to me one of these days." She started off.

"All of you girls are nothing but harlots. You walk around here with your miniskirts and tight pants actin like the world belongs to you. I keep telling my boy that all you girls want to do is use him for whatever y'all can get. But guess what, it's not happening anymore. My son is going to give every last one of you what you deserve. And as long as I'm here, I'm gonna make sure it's done."

I sat there and listened to that crazy ass lady run her mouth nonstop. I was too weak to feed into her shit. Her son just damn near killed me so I needed to regroup. I held my head back down and cried myself to sleep.

I woke up six and a half hours later when I heard Jimmy's voice. "Good morning Mama."

"Good morning baby. How did you sleep?"

"Oh, I slept good." He told her.

"What's for breakfast?"

"I gotta' few boiled eggs in the pot on the stove. And there's still some coffee left so help yourself."

"Is there enough for Pam? He asked.

"Her name is not Pam. Remember she slipped up and said her name was something that started with an L?"

"It's Lynise mama."

"Who cares what it is. You just go in there and get yourself something to eat."

"All right Mama," he replied and then he walked away from her. He had to walk by me to get to the kitchen. So as he passed me, he stopped and kissed me on my forehead. "Good morning, sweet pea. Did you get any sleep?" he smiled

His slimy, wet lips sent an electric shock through my body. Once again I felt violated to the core. Not only did this guy almost kill me again, he forced the organs on the inside of my body to shut down. I urinated and my pants were soaked. The smell coming from my pants was unbearable and I wanted this nightmare to be over. I swear I would've rather had Bishop or the Carter brothers to torture me than to go through this shit. How much more of this am I going to have to take?

Instead of answering his stupid ass question, I turned my focus towards the floor. I couldn't look at him because I wanted to kill him. With the amount of anger and rage I had built up inside of me I could kill him without thinking twice.

"Oh she's being shy, mama." He commented playfully.

"Who cares?!" The old lady replied as she kept her attention glued to the TV.

"Are you hungry?" he continued to question me.

"No," I replied, my voice barely audible.

"You need to hose her down and put her on some clean clothes. Her body is reeking with that pee smell." His mother spoke up.

"Think that dress I took off the other girl will fit her?" he wanted to know.

"You'll never know unless you try." She told him.

At last I was going to get cleaned up. It took for me to almost die and piss on myself for this loser to do something. Damn I wished that the tables were turned. I swear I'd make both of these people pay.

Jimmy wheeled me to the bathroom door. He untied me and carried me into the bathroom over his shoulders. I couldn't feel my legs because they were numb. But I could move my arms.

After Jimmy brought me into the bathroom, he shut the lid of the toilet stool and sat me down on it. He turned on the shower water and held his hand under the spout until he was satisfied with the temperature. "I think this is hot enough." He said.

I didn't comment on it one way or another. At this point, I was helpless. I couldn't say or do anything. I watched this fucking pervert as he stripped me down to nothing and placed me inside of their filthy ass bathtub. And when he started bathing me, I saw the different facial expressions he made when he washed certain parts of my body. For instance, when he washed between my legs and my breasts he'd smile a little bit. It was like he enjoyed it. I could tell that he was getting aroused. And when he started saying that he enjoyed washing me up, I knew that this would be an ongoing thing of his. After I wash you up, I am going to put you in this pretty dress I got saved for you. He said cheerfully.

Finally my shower time was up. He didn't bathe me the way I would've done it but the fact that I was out of those pissy clothes made this trip to the bathroom well worth it. Before we exited the bathroom he wrapped an old towel around me. I thought he was going to put me back in the wheelchair but he didn't. Instead he carried me to a nearby bedroom. Once inside he sat me on the edge of the bed and then he grabbed a blue dress from the closet. "This is going to look pretty on you." He said. He took the towel from my body and threw it on the bed. He didn't have any clean panties for me to put on so I had to go raw dog. After he put the dress on me, he stepped backwards so he could get a better look at me.

"Stand up so I can see how it looks on you." He instructed me.

"I can't move my legs." I told him.

"Well let me help you then." He said and he helped me up from the bed.

He stood me up in front of the mirror and complimented me on how great I looked in this little ass dress. It looked like something that came out of Wal-Mart. Jimmy didn't think so though. He rambled on about how I needed to get my hair fixed and putting on some makeup so I could look pretty for him. I was too weak to make any comments concerning this dress, my hair or some cheap ass makeup. I just wanted him to sit me down and never touch me again.

"Guess what I am going to do for you?" He said all giddy.

"What?" I replied unenthused.

"I am going to put some of mama's lipstick on you so you can look pretty while we are eating breakfast this morning. So whatcha' think about that?" He asked me.

I wanted to tell him to go to hell. But I decided against it. I couldn't handle another episode of him trying to choke the life out of me. So I just left well enough alone.

This fucking maniac put his mother's lipstick on my mouth just like he told me he would. And before we returned to the TV room he cleaned off the wheelchair and strapped me back down in it. As we approached the entryway he announced to his mother that we were coming. "Mama you're going to be so proud when you see what I've done to Lynise."

"I don't care what you've done to her. I told you I don't like her so leave me alone." She said.

"Ahhh, Mama don't act like that. She's gonna be my wife. So it's important to me that you two get along." He pressed the issue.

"Oh hush boy, she ain't no good for you. All she's gonna do is break your heart like the rest of them. Remember we just caught her in a lie less than eight hours ago."

"Mama, I know. But people can change."

"I see you're gonna have to learn the hard way." She stated. She was hell bent on exposing me to her son. This guy has some mental issues so this lady was able to manipulate him without any outside interferences.

I wondered what type of medicine they were taking. Because whatever it was she had to be giving him a double dose of it. One minute Jimmy was walking around here sane and then twenty minutes later he was ready to take my fucking head off. Something just was not adding up.

"You know that when she peed on herself some of it got on the floor?"

"Yes ma'am. I saw it."

"Well good because I'm gonna need you to get it up before I end up slipping and falling on the floor because of it."

"I got it mama. I'm going to get it up after we eat breakfast."

"Is that what you're about to do? Because it looks like you are taking her out of this house with all that lipstick on her lips."

"No mama. I just wanted her to look pretty while we were eating."

"Is that my lipstick on her lips?" she pointed out.

"I used the one that you don't use any more."

"You better not be lying to me boy." She threatened.

"I'm not mama." Jimmy assured her as he continued to push me towards the kitchen. Immediately after we arrived in the kitchen, Jimmy pushed me up to the wobbly kitchen table. He pranced around the kitchen like he was a fucking chef. He pulled a pack of scrapple from the refrigerator and fried it, leaving the edges of it crisp and burnt. The kitchen smelled a hot mess. "Here you go beautiful." He said as he placed the plate of boiled eggs and two slices of well-cooked scrapple in front of me. I scanned the plate for a brief moment and I had to admit that it didn't look half bad. I figured that either I was starving or my eyes were playing tricks on me.

Jimmy sat next to me and fed me until everything on my plate was gone. "Mama, she ate everything I put on her plate." He announced.

"Who cares? I'm going to my room." She told him and left.

Once again Jimmy and I were alone. So this would be a great time to chip away at the wall he built from anyone outside of his mother. But when I thought back to the near death experience that happened after midnight, I convinced myself that it wouldn't be a good idea. What I decided to do was show Jimmy that I was beginning to like him as much as he liked me.

It was evident that those other victims he killed made a lot of bad choices when it pertained to him. Jimmy was looking for acceptance. And I noticed that Jimmy was also looking for love which was something he never got from a woman. His mother has brain washed him into believing that she was the only woman who'd ever love him. But deep down inside of his heart there's a glimmer of hope that he could prove his mother wrong.

"Thank you for breakfast. It was really good."

Jimmy smiled. "You really liked it?" He wondered aloud.

"Yes. It was good."

Jimmy continued to beam. "I'm so glad you liked it. No one ever told me that they liked my cooking but my mama."

"Well good. Then I'll be the first." I smiled back. I swear it was hard to put on this fake smile and act like everything was good. But I had to keep reminding myself that I was in survival mode. And if I was going to get out of here alive, then I had to play their game. Getting Jimmy to turn against his mother is the first thing. And killing him would be the last and final straw.

"Have you ever had a girlfriend?" I asked him.

"One time when I was in high school. But it only lasted a few days and then she dumped me."

"Why did she dump you?"

"Because she wanted me to give her money so she could hang out with her friends. But I didn't have a lot of money to give her. Me and mama were poor. So when I couldn't give her what she wanted, she told me not to talk to her anymore and started dating this other guy in school. I used to see them hug and kiss near the girl's bathroom all the time. And when I would see it, all the other guys and girls used to make fun of me and call me stupid."

"Ahh…really? That wasn't cool."

"I know. She broke my heart."

"What grade were you in when that happened?"

"I was a junior."

"So did you graduate from that school?"

"No. Mama took me out of that school and put me in another school."

"Did you graduate from the new school?"

"Yeah. And mama was proud to."

I forced myself to smile. "That's good. And you should have been proud to."

"I was." He smiled bashfully.

"So how long have you been driving cabs?"

"About ten years now."

"What were you doing before you started driving cabs?"

"I worked as a janitor at the high school I graduated

from. But after working there for eight years I decided to do something easier."

"Have you ever thought about having kids?"

"No. I don't think I'd be a good daddy."

"But, why not?"

"Well because sometimes I slip up and do stupid things. And babies require a lot of work."

"Well don't beat yourself up about it because babies are cute little things and I'm sure if you had one you'd be a good father."

Surprised by my comment he said, "Are you serious? You really think so?"

"Of course, I do. And with the help of your mama, you two would be unstoppable."

Jimmy paused for a second and smiled. It almost seemed like he was trying to look through me or read my mind.

"I knew there was something special about you."

"That's so nice of you to say." I lied. I was saying all the bullshit he wanted to hear. He was soaking it up to.

"Do you have kids?" He questioned me.

"No."

"Why not?"

"Just haven't found the right guy. "

"You think I could be the right guy?"

"It's possible." I said.

"Wow! You sure know how to make a guy feel good." He began to say.

"That's because you deserve it."

"Well, I guess it was meant for me to kill all those girls and get rid of their bodies because if I hadn't I wouldn't have met you."

Stunned by his confession, I asked him how many women did he kill? He thought for a moment and then he said, "Probably around twenty."

After he gave me the number of victims he slaughtered, my heart felt like it had fallen in the pit of my stomach. Was this guy fucking serious? Had he really killed that many women? I was afraid to take this conversation any further. This nut job was crazier than I thought. Killing women came second nature to him. And with his crazy ass mother encouraging him, he'd probably continue to kill until someone stops him. Hopefully that someone would be me.

He reached over and placed his left hand on my left arm. "I'm sorry. Did I spook you?" I held onto my brave face and assured him that I was fine. "Oh no. I'm cool." I lied once again.

"Well, since we're done here. Let me clean up this mess before mama sees it. And then we can take our butts back into the TV room. Who knows we might can catch the rest of Wife Swap." He said and got up from the table.

I watched this weirdo as he wiped down the table and cleaned our dishes. He definitely wanted a normal life but he had no idea that he was going about it wrong.

What the hell am I going to do?

Chapter Thirteen

TRUST NO ONE!

Knowing how Agent Rome and Agent Mann felt about this operation and the safety of Lynise threw my mind into a world wind. I've tried to remain focused while the rest of the agents and I continue to search for Lynise. But with the notion that I have two agents who are totally running interference on my mission to find my witness has made me look at them as enemies. And to know that they don't have any respect for me is really fucking with my ego. Men have it the hardest when we've got to hold our tongues. I'm the HNIC around here, so why don't they get it? And what is this secret that they don't want Lynise to tell? Whatever it is, it will soon come out.

When I came down for breakfast, Agent Mann and Agent Rome were both drinking coffee and talking to Agent Zachary. Everyone except for Agent Rome smiled and spoke to me. After I spoke back, I looked at Rome and said, "Is there are a problem with you and I?"

"I don't think so." He replied.

"So why can't I get a good morning from you?" I

questioned him.

"Because, I'm not having a good morning."

"Well, I guess that answers that."

"Yeah, I guess it did."

I noticed Agent Zachary and Agent Mann looking at one another. I sensed that they felt out of place while Agent Rome and I were going back and forth with each other. So, instead of making it intensely awkward, I poured myself a cup of coffee and exited the kitchen.

I took a seat on the sofa in the TV room and started watching a little bit of the news. I turned up the volume of the TV so that I couldn't hear Agent Rome's voice as much. He and Agent Mann both lost all respect from me. Bottom line.

As I began to get engrossed in the news, Agent Zachary joined me. She took a seat next to me. "Are you alright?" she spoke up first.

"Yeah, I'm good." I lied. But I really didn't want to talk about the fucked up shit concerning Agents Rome and Mann. Both of them are pieces of shit and I wanted to avoid any conversations involving them especially after hearing them make plans to plot against me. I swear that if I didn't have this gun and badge, I'd whip both of their assess and face the consequences later.

"What happened back in the kitchen?"

"Look Zachary, I don't feel like talking about it."

"But don't you think you need to?"

"No I don't.

"But you're the head of this operation, so you've got to communicate with everyone of us."

"Listen, I don't care what I am. If I choose not to communicate to you or anyone else in his house, then that's my prerogative. The main thing everyone in here needs to worry about is finding our witness and getting her back to safety. That's it. I will not entertain any bitching or drama from anyone. Do I make myself clear?"

"Yes. You've definitely made it clear."

"Good. Now let's talk about Mr. Malik Carter. Have the two of you started any dialog? I remember the last time you said that he wanted to take you out to lunch. Have you two talked about when or where you're going?"

"Yes. Last night before I left the club, he told me he wanted to take me to lunch today since I didn't have to work."

"What did you say?"

"I told him sure. So, we're gonna hook up around 1 o'clock."

"Did he say where?"

"Well, he wanted to see where I live. But I told him, I wasn't ready for that. So he finally agreed to meet me at a restaurant called Kincaid's. He said it was in MacArthur mall in downtown Norfolk."

"Okay. That sounds doable."

"Has anything else come up while you've been there?"

Nothing yet. I've noticed that the club has some regulars. You know, smalltime drug dealers and men who have regular jobs and want to stop by for a few drinks before they head home."

"Okay. Well, I guess you're gonna need to get dressed for your hot date." I teased her.

"Oh stop it. You know I'm only doing this for you.

"I know. But be careful. Remember who he's related to."

"Trust me, I'm on guard. But I want to ask you, am I gonna wear a wire?"

"No. I don't see a need to. But I do want you to use your phone to record your whole conversation with."

"Okay. I can do that."

"Sounds like a plan." I said and then I patted her on her thigh. I stood to my feet simultaneously when Agents Mann and Rome walked into the TV room. But somehow they had mistaken it for me trying to avoid them. "You don't have to leave because of us." Agent Rome commented.

"Oh no, that's not what's happening. I was about to leave anyway. Gotta' go hop in the shower so I can start the day." I told him.

"Oh okay." Rome replied.

I wasn't about to get into a pissing match with that bitch ass nigga. So, I excused myself and made my way to the shower.

Before I hopped in the shower, I went into my bedroom to pick out a suit of clothes for today. While I was going through my things I overheard Agent Rome and Agent Mann talking to Agent Zachary about her experience at Club Diamonds. But first they asked her about her upcoming date. "Nervous?" Rome asked.

"Kind of."

"Well, don't be because we're gonna be there watching out for you." Rome assured her.

"I know you will." I heard her say.

"So, how are things at the club otherwise?" Rome probed her.

"Well, it's not as bad as I thought it would be."

"You never mentioned anything about the other girls in the club. Is there a lot of chick fighting going on?"

"Well yeah, the strippers keep a lot of drama going. But other than that, it's just a club of naked women and hard up men throwing money around like their minds are going bad."

"So, when that guy Malik comes around, does he normally stay in his back office, because I remember only seeing him once when Agent Mann and I were there."

"Pretty much. Oh and now that I think about it, I saw a couple of guys going back to his office last night without being escorted by any of the bouncers, which I thought was weird. No one goes behind the stage without being escorted. So when that happened I became a little suspicious."

"Do you think they were the Carter Brothers?"

"I wasn't sure."

"Did they have anything in their hands that looked like it could've been money or drugs?"

"No. They didn't have anything in their hands."

"Hmm… I wonder who they could've been?" I heard Rome say.

"I wanted to ask the bartender who they were but I decided not to because I think she's Malik's watch dog. I've heard a few of the girls in there complain about how certain things go down in the club while Malik isn't there, but yet, he still finds out about it."

"Well, I'm glad you used good judgment. Just do what we tell you to do and we'll handle the rest. And hopefully, your boss upstairs won't have you working this detail too much longer." I heard Rome tell Zachary.

"Hopefully you're right." Zachary replied. I could tell that her heart really wasn't in this. She sounded a bit overwhelmed to say the least. And having Agents Rome and Mann in her fucking ears with a bunch of negative chatter wasn't helping the situation.

I saw through all of that bullshit. Too bad, Zachary didn't. I see that I might be on my own with this operation. That is if Agent Humphreys decides to side with them. If that happens then I'm going to be up a river without a paddle.

When I thought I had heard enough of everyone's bullshit, I headed to the shower. Bathing in some hot water might be the therapy I needed. Who knows, I may even get courageous enough to pistol-whip Agent Rome and Agent Mann and send them back to New Jersey in a UPS box.

It's not like they wouldn't deserve it.

Chapter Fourteen

HATCHING OUT A PLAN

Day five rolled in slowly while I was still strapped down to the fucking wheelchair. I had to face the music that these accommodations were fucked up to the tenth power. The only freedom they gave me was to be able to talk freely without the old rag they had tied around my mouth. Sorry to say that all ended when someone knocked on the front door. My heart rate picked up rapidly. KNOCK, KNOCK, KNOCK.

Jimmy was asleep but after he heard someone knocking on the front door he jumped to his feet. His face looked panic stricken. "Mama, are you expecting someone?" He whispered. His mama was sitting in the love seat a few feet away from me watching TV.

"No. I don't know who that could be."

I watched them closely while they were trying to figure things out. While Jimmy was trying to figure out who was at his front door, his mama turned her sights on me. "Before we do anything, we need to tie her mouth back up before she tries to scream." His mama said.

My heart continued to race at a rapid speed but I held my composure. It was important to convince them that I wouldn't open my mouth. Having my mouth untied would give me a fair advantage to let someone know that I was being held captive. Who knows, it could be the police standing outside the front door. If it was, there was no doubt in my mind that they were coming for me. "You don't have to tie up my mouth. I promise I won't say a word." I whispered. Unfortunately my words meant nothing. Jimmy's mother wrapped that gag around my mouth quicker than I could blink. Immediately after, she instructed Jimmy to watch me while she found out who was at the front door.

By this time, anxiety crept inside my body and engulfed my entire body. *Please, please, please, let it be somebody who'll save me.* I thought to myself. *Lord, I know I have done some bad things but if you get me out of this jam, I will change my life from this day forward.* My thoughts continued. I literally said a small prayer. I just hoped that God heard me.

The person at the door knocked a few more times before Jimmy's mama answered it. "Who is it?" I heard her ask.

"It's the mailman, ma'am. I have a package that I need you to sign." He stated.

"I didn't send for a package." She told him.

"Is your name Mrs. Francis Beckford?" I heard the man yell.

"Yes it is. But I still don't know of any package

that's supposed to come here, so can you just leave it on the porch?"

"No ma'am. I have to get you to sign it." He pressed the issue.

"Well, I'm not in the mood to sign anything right now, so just send it back to where it came from." She replied.

"Okay ma'am. As you wish." He said and then all communication ceased.

When the crazy old lady walked back to the TV room, she looked suspiciously at me. But then she turned her attention to Jimmy. "Do you think that mailman really had something for us?" She asked him.

Jimmy looked puzzled. "If he did, I don't know who it could've came from."

"And neither do I." She said as she sat back down. She got back into her TV show with no problems. Jimmy acted a little paranoid for about an hour or so. But then he calmed himself down and retreated back to doing his own thing.

I sat there feeling sorry for myself. I mean, how in the hell could I have gotten so close to getting someone to help me get out of here? The fucking mailman was right there at their front door. He was right there and now he's gone. What kind of justice am I going to get for myself? It's a crying shame that I have no damn family who'd put out a missing person's report on me. It felt really fucked up to be living in a world and no one really gave a damn about you except for a fucking retard. This guy basically said that we were soul mates. Now how fucked up in the head is he? He and I've never dated. And so far we haven't had sex, so why is it that he cared more about me than the motherfuckers I grew up with or known all my life? Was I that fucked up as a person that nobody liked me? Okay, granted, I've done some messed up shit in my life but I didn't deserve this type of treatment. One minute he and his mama are putting their hands on me, and then the next minute this goof ball is telling me that he loves me. Is this how life will end for me? If so, then kill me now.

"Mama, I'm off to work." Jimmy announced. Since I've been here Jimmy and his mother took shifts to watch me. He'd sit in the TV room with me during the day and she'd watch me at night. It was eleven thirty p.m., so his shift with the cab company was about to begin. "I'm gonna need you to pick up a few things from the store. So, take this list and stop by there on your way home." She told him.

He took the list from her hands and stuffed it in his front shirt pocket. "Be good for mama," he looked at me and said.

"She'd better if she knows what's good for her." His mother commented.

Now of course I wasn't feeling her smartass remark, but what was I supposed to do about it? I couldn't curse her ass out. And I couldn't beat her ass so I just chalked it up and reminded myself that I'd have my way with her one of these damn days.

Jimmy eventually made his way out the front door. His mother sat in her usual spot and turned the TV channel to the news. Under normal circumstances I hated to watch the news channels. I had no interest in the local news. But now I've become obsessed. While the old lady kept up with the weather and the local news I was doing the same thing, minus the weather.

The old lady and I heard about the big lay off at the Portsmouth Shipyard, the increase in tolls and then the segment about the serial killing came on. My heart skipped a beat when the reporter stated that the homicide detectives have been getting a lot of tips but no arrests have been made.

From the second the reporter started talking I noticed that my heart started beating at an irregular pace. But when she announced that no arrest had been made I felt a load of shit starting to weigh down on my shoulders. "Tonight Newport News police are still looking for two women that went missing a few weeks ago and the person or persons responsible for it. They said they have some strong leads. One of those leads involved a witness who said they last saw one of those women get into a taxi cab. Now while that may be a good tip the police are still asking that if anyone has anymore information on the whereabouts of either of these women to please contact the tip line at 1-888-LOCKUUP."

After the reporter ended the broadcast, the old lady got up from her seat. "I don't want to hear a peep out of you." She said and then she left the TV room. She returned a couple minutes later with a cell phone in her hand. Immediately after she sat back down she got Jimmy on the line. "Hey son, I think we got a problem." She said.

"What's going on?" I heard him ask. The volume on her phone was up really high. The only reason for that would be because she needed a hearing aid.

"I just saw the news. And they're reporting that they got a witness saying that they saw one of those girls get into a cab."

"Did they give the name of the cab? Or say what color it was?" he wanted to know.

"If they did, the news reporter didn't mention it."

"Well good. Then I guess we have nothing to worry about."

"Look son, I just want you to be careful out there. You never know who's out there watching."

"Mama, I'm a big boy. I can handle anything that comes my way." I heard him say.

"Okay. Well, call me in a couple of hours just so I'll know that you're all right."

"Sure I can do that."

"I love you."

"I love you too."

When the old lady disconnected the call from Jimmy she sat the phone by her side and continued to watch

TV. I went back to watching TV as well. But I couldn't stop from thinking about how she was telling him to be careful. She acted like he was the one in harms way. Was she fucking smoking crack or something? I mean, really lady!

Please wake up and smell the fucking coffee.

In addition to the drama surrounding this lady warning Jimmy to be careful, I also couldn't shake the fact that there was a possible witness that saw one of those girls get into a cab. Now I'm left to wonder about whether or not this information would eventually lead back to Jimmy's psychotic ass? Will they put two and two together and bust his ass? I need a huge miracle. This guy needs a jail cell with two beds for he and his mother.

Where is the Justice?

Chapter Fifteen

HAVING COCKTAILS

I sat at the bar of the restaurant Kincaid's when Agent Zachary and Malik walked in. She was all smiles and so was Malik. Seeing this guy Malik for the first time in broad daylight was quite surprising. Mr. Carter stood at a modest height for a man. His build was quite impressive. I could definitely tell that he worked out. But what caught my eye was his jewelry collection. In my mind a strip club owner and especially one who's related to a couple of notorious gangsters, would wear a lot of flashy jewelry. The guys in the rap videos wore some very expensive diamond jewelry, so I would imagine that a black club owner would mimic their behavior. Sorry to say I was wrong. Malik had on a gold, presidential Rolex watch and one diamond and gold pinky ring. It was nothing extravagant. But everyone that saw him knew he lived well.

The restaurant's host escorted them both to their table. I watched him while he watched Agent Zachary's ass switch from side to side. There was no doubt what he had on his mind. After the host handed them both menus he left them alone to look over their menus.

Not too long after the host left, a waiter greeted them and took their drink orders. When he returned he had a glass of Chardonnay and a couple shots of Grand Marnier in a wine glass. Halfway through their cocktails the waiter brought them back their meals. I noticed that Agent Zachary had shrimp tossed in pasta while Malik had a grilled chicken breast with some brown sauce poured over it and a side of yellow rice. Both of their meals looked great. So, while they were eating away, Malik got a call on his cell phone. He excused himself from the table and walked out of the restaurant and into the mall. The moment he went out of sight, I looked back at Agent Zachary. She returned the look and hunched her shoulders like she didn't know what was going on. She and I sat in our seats and waited patiently for his return.

One minute passed. Then two minutes passed. And then five minutes passed. And there was still no Malik. I was very curious to see what was taking him so fucking long to get back to the table with Agent Zachary. I paid the bartender for my tab and then I slid off the barstool. As soon as I exited the restaurant I saw Malik take a small plastic bag from a young guy who looked to be every bit of 19-years-old, if not younger and walked off. I wanted so desperately to know what was in the bag but I wasn't there to build a drug case against Malik. I was only interested in getting information that could possibly help me find Lynise. Everything else was secondary.

Malik passed me on his way back into the restaurant. I, on the other hand, was interested in seeing where that young guy was going. I ended up following him to the parking garage where a late model, white Range Rover with dark tinted windows was waiting for him.

It seemed like everything happened so fast because as soon as he got inside the truck, it pulled off into the sunset. The only problem I had with this was that I wasn't close enough to the truck to see the driver. I was so close, but yet so far away.

Luckily, I was able to rebound by taking a couple of screen shots of the license plate with my cell phone while the truck was driving away. I planned to check on the plate when I got back to the safe house. Who knows, I may get a good hit.

I got into my car and sat there for a moment trying to figure out what I was going to do next. I couldn't leave the mall because Agent Zachary was still having lunch with that Malik guy. I also knew that I couldn't go back into the restaurant for fear that I'd stick out like a sore thumb. Malik would spot me immediately.

After careful thinking, I decided to stay in my car and wait for Agent Zachary and Malik to leave so I could follow her back to the safe house. It was imperative that I kept a close watch on Agent Zachary. After hearing Agents Mann and Rome talk shit about me to Agent Zachary, I felt it was my duty to make her feel less stress as possible. Who knows she may be my ticket to finding Lynise. And if she isn't, then I'm going to have to move forward with another plan. Either way, I had to protect her.

It seemed like it was taking forever for Agent Zachary to end her date with Malik. I was becoming impatient because I wanted to get back to the safe house so I could log into the DMV database and find out who the license plate on the white Range Rover was registered to. I became so anxious that I called Agent Humphreys.

"I need you to look up a plate for me," I started off saying.

"What's the state?"

"Virginia."

"What's the plate number?"

"Echo-Bravo-Oscar-2891," I said.

"Okay. Give me a minute." He replied and then he fell silent. "Was that plate on a 2012 white Range Rover?" Humphreys asked.

"Yes," I told him.

Five seconds later, he said, "You are not going to believe this."

"Tell me." I said anxiously.

"This vehicle is registered to Terrence Carter."

"Get the fuck out of here! You're kidding me right?" I replied with excitement.

"No way, buddy. I am serious as a heart attack." Humphreys commented.

"What city is the vehicle registered in?"

"Virginia Beach."

"What's the address?"

"5391 Pleasure House Road."

I grabbed an ink pen from the cup holder in the car and wrote down the address. Before the day ended, I was going by this address to see if I could finally put a face with the last name Carter. I was ready to see who wanted Lynise dead.

Agent Zachary finally ended her lunch date with Malik. He walked her to her car, which was on the 1st floor of the parking garage. I was parked on the opposite side of the garage, but I was still able to see the car. Seconds after Malik kissed Agent Zachary on the cheek, he opened her car door and closed it after she sat down in the driver's seat. He said a few words to her as she drove her car in reverse. And when she put the car in drive he watched her until she drove away.

To avoid from bringing heat to Agent Zachary or myself, I exited the parking garage of the mall on the side where I was parked. And as soon as I paid the toll clerk, I dialed Agent Zachary's cell phone number and raced towards Monticello Avenue. She answered on the first ring. "Hello," she said.

"Are you okay?" I asked her.

"Yes, I'm fine. I'm just glad that it's finally over."

"What took you so long?"

"I couldn't stop him from touching my hands and talking me to death."

"Did he mention anything about why it took him so long to get back into the restaurant?"

"All he did was apologize and say that he had to meet with someone in the mall."

"Well yeah, he met some young thug. And I caught the thug handing him a plastic bag. I couldn't tell what was in it. But right after Malik took the bag, he and the guy parted ways."

"Did you see where the guy went?"

"Yeah, I followed him into the parking garage and saw him get into a white Range Rover. I got Agent Humphreys to run the license plate number and come to find out that the vehicle is registered to a Terrence Carter."

"Get the fuck out of here! You're kidding right?!"

"No, I am not. And I've got a physical address to prove it."

"So, what are you gonna do with it?"

"I'm gonna go by there and see if I can put a face to the name."

"You're not going over there alone are you?"

"No. You're going with me." I replied nonchalantly.

"Do you think that this is a good idea?"

"Sure I do. Now tell me where you are so we can meet up."

"I just merged onto Highway 264."

"Okay. Drive slowly because I'm coming that way too."

"How can I drive slow on the highway?"

"Okay. Well, do the speed limit and stay in the far right lane until I catch up to you." I instructed her.

"Why don't I get off the next exit and wait for you?"

"Alright. Well, do that and I'll see you in about five minutes."

"Okidoki." She said.

Finding Agent Zachary was fairly easy. She was parked in the parking lot of the Hardee's restaurant awaiting my arrival. I pulled up next to her rented vehicle and rolled down the driver's side window. I smiled at her. "Why are you so happy?" she asked.

"It feels like I just won the freaking lottery or something."

"Well, what's the game plan Mr. Lottery Winner?"

"I was thinking it would be a good idea if you left your rental car here and climbed in the car with me. But then I figured it wouldn't make sense to drive all the way back down here after we left Virginia Beach. So, why don't you follow me and when we get close to the house, I'll give you further instructions from there.

"Okay. Cool. Let's do that." She agreed.

I keyed in the home address of Terrence Carter into my GPS device and a couple of seconds later, the directions popped on the screen. As I drove out of the Hardee's parking lot Agent Zachary followed. It took us approximately twenty minutes to drive from Norfolk to the Virginia Beach address.

The neighborhood was called Mason Brick Estates and it was beautiful hands down. The homes here had to be in the ballpark of one million and up. The only amenity missing was that the community wasn't gated.

I pulled over to the side of the street and motioned for Agent Zachary to pull her car beside mine. "What's up?" she said after she rolled down her window.

"According to my GPS, the house is located two blocks up and then make a right onto Pleasure House Road. After you make a right, drive slowly and tell me if the white Range Rover is parked outside."

"What if someone's outside?"

"Just act normal and look like you're lost. As a matter of fact, call me now so I can talk you through it." I said calmly. I needed her to know that I was in this thing with her.

She took a deep breath and then she exhaled. "Here goes nothing." She said as she began to drive away.

"Call me now." I yelled.

"I'm doing it now." She yelled back.

One second later my cell phone rang. "Are you up here?" she asked.

"Yes, I'm up here."

"Okay well, I'm putting you on speaker right now."

"Alright. But keep your phone low so no one sees it."

"Foster, I know. Please be quiet because you're making me nervous."

"Okay. I won't say anything else. But you've got to communicate with me as soon as you get close to the house."

"Okay. I'm making the right turn now." She said. "What's the numbers on the house?"

"It's 5391."

"Oh.... Okay." She said and then she went silent. "Foster, I see it." She blurted out. I could tell by her voice that her heart rate picked up.

"Do you see the white Range Rover?"

"Yes, I see it. It's in the driveway. And it's parked next to a black Aston Martin."

"What color is the house? How big is it?" I pressed her with more questions.

"It's a brick house and the bricks are a dark mahogany color. It's two stories and it is massive."

"What kind of window treatments do they have? Can you see inside the house from your car?"

"Oh shit! Somebody is coming out of the house."

"Who is it?"

"If this Terrence Carter guy is brown skin and tall then I see our guy. Shit! He's looking directly at me." She replied, her voice cracking.

"Agent Zachary.....calm down! What is the matter with you? You aren't acting like an undercover agent right now." I snapped.

"I know. I know. It's just that I don't want to blow my cover." She whispered like someone would hear her.

"Listen, just act like you're looking for someone's house. You know, stop the car at the house two doors down from his house and then drive away. And if you want to do it again, drive a little ways up the block and stop in front of another house and then drive off again."

"Okay, that's what I'll do." She said, a little more confident.

"While you're doing that, can you still see him?"

"No. I think he might've gotten into one of the cars."

"And where are you?"

"I'm like three houses away from his."

"Look in the rearview mirror and tell me if you can see him now."

"No. I don't see him."

"Well, slow down at the next house you come to and see if you can see his house from there."

"Oh shit! There he goes. I see him coming down the street behind me."

"Alright Agent Zachary. Calm down. Don't move. Keep your foot on the brake and act like you're looking at the house."

"Okay." I heard her say and then she sighed heavily.

"Where is he? Has he passed you yet?"

"He's coming now." She replied, sounding a bit alarmed.

"Remember what I said. Be calm...." I began to coach her but then she cut me off.

"No, I'm looking for 5406 Pleasure House Road. I'm beginning to think that I have the wrong address." I heard her say.

"You're absolutely right because there is no 5406 Pleasure House Road. So, you may want to call the person you're looking for and tell them you're lost." I heard a male's voice say, even though it was kind of faint.

"I'm gonna do just that." Agent Zachary replied.

"Good luck." I heard the guy say.

"Thank you." Agent Zachary said.

I waited a few minutes before I spoke. I wanted to make sure the coast was clear. Thankfully Agent Zachary spoke first. "He's gone." She said.

"Which way is he going?" I asked her.

"He's making a left on the next street so he's coming back your way."

"Has he turned the corner yet?"

"He's doing it now so you may wanna duck down in your seat."

"I'm on it as we speak." I told her. Instead of ducking down in my seat I leaned the driver's side chair back. This helped me to still be able to see Mr. Carter as he drove by my car.

Like clockwork Mr. Carter came rolling in my direction. My windows were semi tinted, so I had another way of being obscured from anyone outside the car. After he rolled by, I spoke into the receiver of my cell phone. "He just rolled by." I said.

"What do we do now?" Agent Zachary asked me.

"We're gonna go back to the safe house."

"Roger that."

Chapter Sixteen

THE FOLLOWING NIGHT

Despite the warning that Jimmy's mother gave him the night before after seeing the news segment, Jimmy felt like he was untouchable. He bragged about getting away with all the lives he had taken. This guy was a fucking monster. I mean, unprecedented.

Jimmy came in the TV room after he got ready for work. He had three hours to hang around the house until his shift started. I was in my usual spot, strapped down to the wheelchair only a few feet away from the TV. "Mama, how do I look? Think I can pick up another hot date tonight?" he asked. He twirled around in the middle of the floor like he was a fucking Calvin Klein model. He looked a fucking mess, displaying an old button down shirt, a pair of khaki pants and a busted pair of loafers.

His mother was sitting in her favorite chair watching TV. "What hot date? I thought you said she was the one?" she replied nonchalantly, after she took her eyes off the TV screen and looked at him from head to toe.

"She is mama. But I just don't want to put all my eggs in one basket just in case she screws me over."

"I'm glad you're finally talking with some sense. But I don't think it's a good idea for you to go out there and mess with anymore of those girls. I told you last night that that reporter said that those cops got some tips that came in their office. So, don't go out there and do something stupid. Leave those girls alone for right now. Let the cops think that you aren't out there roaming their streets anymore. And then they'll forget all about you."

"Mama, I was just kidding. I'm not messing around with none of those girls tonight."

"Thank goodness."

Jimmy walked over to me and kissed me on my forehead. "I was just teasing a few minutes ago so don't pay any attention to what I said. You are my one and only love. And as soon as the time is right, I'm gonna give you the ring my daddy gave to my mama and then we're gonna get married." He told me. I wanted to vomit in my fucking mouth. His wet kisses were the worst thing ever. His lips felt like an old mildewed washcloth.

"Oh leave her alone. Will you?!" she spat. She sounded irritated.

"But I'm in love mama. I've never loved a woman like I love her."

"Boy, you don't know what love is."

"Yes, I do."

"Then tell me," she instructed him.

"Love is when you can't do without someone. And that's how I feel about her." He explained.

"Well you go ahead and continue to act like you're in love and I'm gonna go in my bedroom, so I can get some peace and quiet." She told him and then she stood to her feet.

Immediately after she took her first step she slipped and fell down to the floor. "Awwwwwww," she screamed.

Jimmy rushed to her side. "Oh my God mama, are you alright?"

"I think I broke my hip," she said. I could tell that she was in pure agony as she laid on her right side.

Very concerned, Jimmy said, "Come on mama, let me help you get off the floor."

"Awwwwwww," she screamed louder while Jimmy tried to pull her up from underneath both of her arms. "It's not going to work, so just leave me laying here," she told him.

"No, I won't do that. I'm gonna use all of my strength to lift you up." He told her.

"No, son it's not gonna work. You're gonna have to call a paramedic. " She managed to say while she cried out to Jimmy.

"Oh no mama, you know we can't let nobody in here. Remember we got Lynise sitting right there."

"Well, why don't you think of a better way to get me off the floor.

"Mama, you're gonna have to trust me. So when I

say lift I want you to press your weight against me."

"But it's not gonna work son."

"Yes it is mama. You got to trust me." He said, in a coaching manner.

I sat back and smiled. I can honestly say that I was enjoying seeing Jimmy's mother in all that pain. I was enjoying it so much, his mother saw me smiling and she nearly spit fire at my ass.

"Jimmy look at her. She's laughing in our faces." She pointed out while she cried. She was seething at the mouth. She was so furious with me that I could see smoke coming from her ears. She was not a happy camper at all.

Jimmy wasn't too happy to see a smirk on my face either. But at this point, I could care less how they saw me. I was the fucking victim not her. Shit! If he had left me where I was then I wouldn't be here to start with. Much less be in her face and laughing at her old miserable ass!

Jimmy stood to his feet. He got in my face and literally spit venom. "You think that this is funny?"

"No." I lied. But he didn't buy it.

And that's when he lunged back and hurled a back handed slap against my face. It seemed like my entire left jaw had cracked. Pain crippled me that instant. I grabbed that side of my face and screamed to the top of my voice. "Fuck you and your mama! I am so tired of y'all! I hope the bitch never walks again!" I roared.

But that outburst didn't help me at all. Before I even

realized it, Jimmy had hurled more blows to my face. He knocked me into oblivion. "You think you can talk about my mama and I don't do anything about it? Bitch, are you crazy? I love my mama! And you think I'm gonna let you sit here and disrespect her?" He snapped.

Jimmy hit me so many times, I had completely lost track. I felt my face starting to get numb. And his words became one big blur. And there was nothing I could do about it.

I did, however, hear when Jimmy's mother begged him to stop hitting me. I believed that if she hadn't said a word, this guy would've beat me until I was a dead. Lucky me!

"Son, look at your hands." I heard his mother say.

"I know mama. I know."

"You gotta go and wash them off." She instructed him, while she continued to cry.

I had no idea if she was crying because she felt bad for me, or if she was still in a lot of pain. I swear, I didn't know what to think anymore.

Jimmy had beat me pretty bad. I knew he had blacked both of my eyes because I could barely see out of them. I was able to see him walk in the direction of the kitchen. Seconds later, I heard the faucet water running. So I knew he was trying to wash the blood off. And here I set, helplessly.

A few moments later, Jimmy returned from the kitchen. He walked back in the room drying his hands with a handful of paper towels.

"Jimmy you're gonna have to come out of that bloody shirt too."

"Never mind that. I'm more concerned with getting you off the floor."

"Will you please take off that shirt? It's making me nauseous just looking at it."

"Fine mother." He said and ripped the shirt off his back. He threw the shirt down to the floor and took another shot at getting her off the floor. Doing it without causing her severe pain was not an option. She cried with every pull and tug.

"Jimmy this is not going to work." She cried harder.

"But it has to mama." He became persistent.

"Honey, I know you don't want to hear this, but you're gonna have to call the paramedics."

"Listen baby, this is what we can do," she started off saying, "You can put the gag back around her mouth and put her in the back laundry room. And then when you're done, you can come back in here and clean up all that blood off the floor and change into another pair of pants and a shirt. And those paramedics ain't gon' know the difference." She concluded.

Jimmy stood there for a minute, thinking about what his deranged ass mother said. She must've convinced him that he could pull off the ultimate scam because he grabbed the handles of my wheelchair and began to roll my ass out of the TV room.

The laundry room was dark and had a damp like smell. It wasn't unbearable, but it stood out. Keep in mind I couldn't see a thing. But the drops of blood dripping from my face down to my chest made me painfully aware of what had just happened to me. At this very moment, I just wanted to die. It seems like I've been running for my life as long as I can remember. And today I can honestly say that I am tired. I'm tired of living and breathing. And I won't fight anymore. At least this way I can finally get some rest.

While I sat there with the desire to just wither away, I heard a lot of rumbling around in the other room.

"Did you call them yet?" I heard his mother ask.

"Mama let me get the rest of his blood off the floor and I will call them."

"But, I don't know how much longer I can lay on the floor like this."

"Okay Mama. I'm gonna call them now."

A minute or so passed and I heard Jimmy speaking with a 911 operator. He put the call on speaker so the operator could hear his mother speak. "My mama fell on the floor and she thinks she broke her hip."

"How do you know she broke her hip?" The woman asked.

"She's right here so I'm gonna let you talk to her."

"Ma'am, are you on the phone?" The operator asked.

"Yes, I'm here."

"What's your name ma'am?"

"My name is Mrs. Francis Beckford."

"Alright Mrs. Beckford, can you tell me what happened?"

"Yes. I got up from the chair in my TV room and when I tried to step away, I tripped and fell down on my hip. And it hurts so bad, so that's why I think I broke it."

"What is your address?" The woman kept questioning Jimmy's mother.

"I'm at 842 Ocean View Avenue."

"Okay. Just stay where you are and I will have a paramedic to you in a few minutes.

"I will, thank you." Mrs. Beckford replied.

After Jimmy's mother hung up the phone she instructed him to get her purse from her bedroom. I heard Jimmy scurry down the hallway.

A few moments later, he scurried back down the hallway and into the room. "Here mama, I got your purse."

"Just put it on the chair so I won't forget it when the paramedics take me out of here."

"Okay mama, I'm setting it right here." I heard him say.

Once again, I couldn't see anything but I heard the loud sirens blaring from the paramedics. I even heard sirens blaring from a fire truck. And for the first time, a small tab of hope came over me. Was I finally about to be rescued? Was this my chance to live and breathe again? Or was I fooling myself? Whenever it happens, I won't be able to control it.

I started hearing at least three different sets of footsteps. And then voices came immediately after. "Where is she?" The first male voice asked.

"She's in the TV room." Jimmy replied.

"Yes, I'm back here." She yelled.

"From one to ten, and ten being the worst, how bad is the pain?" The same male voice asked.

"It's an eight." She told him.

"Can you move?" Another voice asked.

"No. My son tried to pick me up a few times but it didn't work. My hip was hurting too bad. So I told him to leave me alone and call you guys."

"Okay. Well we're gonna all lift you up at the same time and put you on this gurney. Now keep in mind this is going to hurt but the quicker we get you to the hospital, the faster we can get you feeling better."

"I don't care. I just want to get this pain to stop."

"Ma'am, we will take care of you. Now when we count to three we're gonna all lift you up, so take a deep breath."

"Okay. " I heard her say, but it was more like a soft cry.

Without another moment's notice, the men counted loudly and when they got to the number three I heard an agonizing scream and I knew they had lifted her into the air and laid her down on the gurney. Her cries became more and more intense. She made sure they knew that she was in a lot of pain.

"Okay the hard part is over. Now we're going to get you to the hospital." One man said.

"Is she allergic to anything?" Another man asked.

"No. She's not allergic to anything." Jimmy replied.

"Sounds great. Now are you going to follow us to the hospital?" One of the familiar voices asked.

"Yes. I'm going to get some of her things and I will be right behind you." Jimmy said. They didn't know it, but he was trying to rush them out of the house. And I knew, that if that happened, God knows when I'd have another chance at getting out of here.

"Okay, Well, I'm gonna help Jason, put this nice lady into the ambulance. And then Chuck and I are going to head back to the fire station." One of the men said.

"Alright, thanks Nick."

"Don't mention it." Nick said and then I heard a couple of footsteps leaving the house.

I felt the pressure mounting on my shoulders, because it sounded like there was only one man left in the house. So the first thought that popped in my head was to make some noise, some kind of way. But how was I going to do that when I couldn't see what was around me? It was pitch black. So the second thought popped in my head, telling me to try and make some noise with my mouth. Now I knew it would be somewhat impossible since my mouth had been tied up, but hey, I wouldn't know if it would work if I didn't try it. Here goes nothing, I said to myself.

"Help… Help…. Help…. Help," I screamed, even though my words were muffled. But no one heard me because after I stopped, I heard one of the paramedics still carrying on a conversation with Jimmy.

Next, I used the weight of my body to rock the wheelchair back and forth. And while I was rocking the wheelchair I began to scream again.

I rocked the wheelchair back and forth so hard that I managed to fall sideways onto the floor. Boom!

It felt like the whole laundry room shook. Thankfully, the loud noise from my fall got the attention of the paramedic that stayed in the house to talk to Jimmy.

"Did you hear that?" I heard the man ask.

"Yeah. That was probably my cat knocking over something in the laundry room." Jimmy lied.

"No….. No….. He's lying!" I screamed once more. But again my words were muffled. So I started kicking my feet. And what do you know my feet struck the washing machine. It was like music to my ears.

"Wait a minute sir, that's not a cat back there. Are you hiding something back there?" The man asked.

"No sir. That's my cat."

"Don't lie to me sir. Now tell me, if you've got somebody back there?" The man demanded.

While he was demanding that Jimmy give him a truthful answer, I continued to kick the washing machine. I was not about to let this man get out of this house without saving me.

Suddenly I heard footsteps walking in my direction. I wanted to be optimistic but I couldn't. Nothing in my life ever went the way I wanted it to. I was plagued with bad karma. So, why would it be different this time?

"Don't go back there." I heard Jimmy warn the paramedic.

So I kept kicking my feet against the washing machine.

"I'm warning you. Now I told you not to go back there." Jimmy said again.

But the guy kept walking to where I was.

My heart was racing uncontrollably. I finally felt like there was a light at the end of the tunnel. And what do you know I finally saw that light. My eyes nearly popped out of my head when the door to the laundry room opened. The light from the hallway illuminated as the white guy stood before me. He was more shocked than I was. "What the fuck is going on? Why do you have her tied up? And why is she so fucking bloody?" His questions came one after the other.

I started crying all over again. But there was no way you could see my tears from all of the blood painted on my face. "Please help me!" I begged, even though he couldn't understand what I was saying with this fucking gag. But as it turned out, he needed the help when he reached down to take the gag from my mouth, Jimmy walked up behind him, aimed a gun at the paramedic's head and blew him into pieces. This man's entire skull exploded like it was a fucking pumpkin. All the human tissue connected to his brains splattered on me and on everything in the laundry room. I started kicking and screaming after the paramedics' dead body fell on top of me. "See what you made me do." Jimmy screamed and kicked me.

"Aggh!" I shrieked. Instinctively my hands flew up to my head in an attempt to stop his blows from landing in my face. I tried to curl into a fetal position as his boot slammed into my abdomen, then with the force of a wrecking ball the boot slammed into my rib cage.

"My mama was right. You ain't no different from the rest of those girls."

"What's going on? Did I hear a gunshot?" I heard the other paramedic yell as he rushed down the hall towards us. Jimmy immediately turned around and aimed his gun at the other paramedic. Without a moments notice, he shot the gun until he ran out of bullets.

After the gunshots stopped, I heard the front door slam shut. "Oh fuck! He got away." Jimmy panicked. "Shit! What am I going to do?" He screamed as he punched the wall in the hallway. But then something popped in his head because right after he punched the wall, he took off and ran down the hallway. "Fuck! He just drove off with mama." Jimmy roared. I heard the vengeance in his tone. So, I knew he was about to unleash the beast inside of him.

I heard him slam the front door shut and then I heard

him as he stormed back down the hallway. When he reappeared in the doorway of the laundry room, he looked down at me. "This is all your fault. You sneaky bitch! I should've raped and killed you when I let you get in my cab. But no, I had to be good and bring you home to my mama so we could all be a family. Yeah, you screwed me over. So I'm going to pay you back real good after I get us out of here."

Once Jimmy figured out that he didn't have much time to get out of here, he lifted the dead paramedics' body off me and then he wheeled me out of the laundry room. I was still covered in blood and lacerations, but Jimmy wasn't concerned about that. He was focused on getting out of here before the other paramedic called the police to the house. I had no idea how he was going to execute his escape. But I was fully aware that he had no intentions of leaving me behind. "If you take me with you, I'm only gonna slow you down." I got up the courage to say.

"Shut the fuck up before I kill you right now!" he screamed.

Chapter Seventeen
I Can't Blow My Cover

I arrived to the strip club about thirty minutes before Agent Zachary was scheduled to come in. I sat in the far right corner of the club, bought a beer and began to watch the show that this black stripper was putting on.

Unconsciously, I looked down at my watch at least seven times within the first fifteen minutes that I was there. I was on edge still wondering where the hell was Lynise? And how come I and the other agents hadn't been able to find her? Had her life already been taken? I hadn't told the other agents, but I was slowly loosing hope in finding her alive.

While I sipped on my beer, I noticed a couple of guys on the other side of the club swapping money for drugs. From where I sat, it looked like it was only an ounce or two of marijuana. After the buyer smelled the product, he stuffed it on the inside of his jacket and made a toast with the guy that he gave the money to.

After that exchange I witnessed a couple of the strippers giving a couple of the guys lap dances. The rap music was booming from the D.J. booth. The girls loved it.

I rocked my head to the beat and continued to sip on my beer when this very beautiful woman approached me. She looked like Evelyn Lozada from Basketball Wives twin sister. She had Evelyn's body and all. She gave me a huge smile. Can I give you a lap dance?

"What's your name?"

"Hollywood." She said seductively, biting on the tip of her finger.

"Well Hollywood, as much as I want to be in your company, right now isn't a good time." I told her.

"Why not? You look lonely over here all by yourself. Don't you want some company?"

"Listen baby girl, you are as beautiful as they come. But I'm not in the mood for a lap dance right now." I explained to her.

"Are you depressed or something? Because if you are, I can take your mind off of it." She pressed the issue.

I smiled at her because she was becoming relentless. She was definitely a hustler. And if my circumstances dealing with Lynise were different I would've loved for this chick to ride my dick. "Hey look, Sunshine, I've got a lot on my mind, and all I want to do is sit here and relax. Now if for some reason, I start feeling better then I'll call you back over here."

"Okay. Cool." She said then she walked away.

I watched as she made her way back across the floor, and I had to admit that she was sexy as hell. That chick had a body out of this fucking world. And to see her strutting that fat ass she had started getting my dick hard, which was why I declined her offer. Having her grind on me would've fucked my head up and I would not have been focused when Agent Zachary clocked in. I needed to be on guard at all times.

Once I had guzzled down my beer, I got the waitress to give me another one. I had to act like I was a bonafide patron and not an undercover agent. So, after the young lady handed me my second beer, I screwed the top off and took my first sip. And while I'm doing this I see someone coming towards me through my peripheral vision. I turned around to see who it was and it was Malik, the owner of the club and two of his bouncers. I gave him a fake ass smile and waited to hear what he had to say.

He extended his hand and welcomed me to the club. I shook his hand and thanked him for acknowledging my patronizing. But he threw me for a loop when he told me that he'd been watching me and noticed that every time I came to his club I'd drink a couple of beers but I always avoided his dancers and never interacted with anyone in the club but his new waitress. I swear, while this guy laid out every detail of my movements in his club, I got shook. This guy literally made me feel uncomfortable. I was an agent for God's sake. No one has ever made me feel this much anxiety in one sitting.

So quite naturally I had to defuse any suspicions he may have had. But most importantly, I had to get the heat off of Agent Zachary because she was about to walk through those doors at any moment.

"Listen sir, first of all, your dancers and your waitresses are gorgeous, which is why I come here. But as far as who I interact with in here is pure coincidental. I told Ms. Hollywood that she was beautiful and sexy when she asked me if I wanted a lap dance. I also told her that I was going through something personal and that I wasn't interested in a lap dance at this very moment. And if my mood starts to change before I left out of here that I would call on her personally."

"Are you sure you ain't no cop? Because you give off the vibe that you're a cop." Malik questioned me.

"No, I'm not a cop." I replied.

"Well, you know that if you are a cop and someone asks you that question, you gotta tell them the truth?"

"I think I've heard that somewhere." I told him. I tried to be as cool as I could be.

"So, you're not a cop?" Malik pressed on.

"Nope. I am not a cop." I said, trying to be as convincing as I could.

"Well, since you're not a cop then it would be okay if I pat you down?"

Knowing that this guy wasn't going to leave me alone had me feeling uneasy. I never traveled without my badge and my government issued 9mm Glock. So I was in a tight spot. "Do I have any options?" I wanted to know.

"Yeah. If you want to stay here then I have the right to search you. But if me searching you is a problem then you're gonna have to leave my club." He told me. And from what I could see, this guy was serious.

It didn't take me long to figure out what I wanted to do. So I immediately, did the latter. I placed my half empty bottle of beer on the table, stood to my feet and told this guy and his henchmen to have a nice night. I was out of his club in a matter of five seconds.

"I told you that nigga was a cop." One of his bouncers blurted out.

"He's a bitch ass nigga too!" I heard Malik comment.

They made it blatantly obvious that they wanted to start some shit with me. But I let their bogus ass tactics go over my head. I wasn't going to let them blow my cover. I didn't need the heat.

On my way out of the club, I happened to see Agent Zachary walking towards me. And right when I was getting ready to greet her, she yelled and said, "Malik, don't tell me I'm getting a grand welcome."

I had to give it to her because she was on her A-game. The fact that she realized I was about to speak to her and she prevented me from doing so by taking control of the situation, and warning me that Malik was standing at the front door watching me leave was amazing.

I heard the door of the club close after Agent Zachary greeted Malik. That was my cue to get off his property and get in my car. This way, I had a little more control of my surroundings. Back in my car I immediately called Agent Humphreys while I watched a ton of men and women come and go from the club. This scene would make for a great reality show.

"Humphreys stay by the phone because I may need you to come out here."

"What's going on?"

"I was just escorted out of the strip club by the owner and two of his bouncers."

"What happened?"

"I was either spotted on their cameras or someone told the owner that all the times I have come there that I don't interact with the strippers and that I only dealt with his new waitress."

"He was talking about Zachary, huh?"

"Yeah, he was. So after he got through with all the preliminaries he popped the question and asked me if I was a cop? I told him no. But me telling him that I wasn't a cop didn't go over well because a couple of seconds later he wanted to know if he could pat me down. And of course I told him that he couldn't and that's when he told me to get out of his establishment."

"Where are you now?" Humphreys asked. He seemed alarmed by what I was saying.

"I'm outside sitting in my car watching all the traffic going in and out of the club."

"Think you might need some back up?"

"I'm good for now. But keep your phone by you just in case."

"Did Zachary see the incident between you and Malik?"

"No. She hadn't come in yet. She's in there now though."

"Do you think it's safe for her to be in there? Remember you said he knew she only dealt with you."

"Yeah, I know. But, I think she'll be good. She's a smart agent. So, if it gets hot in there she'll let us know."

"Has anything else capped off out there?" Humphreys wanted to know.

"Well so far, I've only seen a few drug deals go down. Nothing big. The guys that come to this club are small time dealers."

"Okay. But call me if you need me."

"Don't worry I will."

I hung up with Agent Humphreys and began my surveillance outside the club since I was kicked out of it. I looked down at my watch and realized that tonight was going to be a long night, especially since Agent Zachary just started her shift. Hopefully, I'd see some action outside. I didn't want to see anyone get hurt but any kind of entertainment amongst niggas from the street would do. Either the guys are standing around disrespecting women by putting their hands on them and calling them bitches or the women are getting in the men's faces and calling them deadbeats and threatening to call the police on them.

Only in America!

Chapter Eighteen
HOW WILL I SURVIVE THIS?

Jimmy raced around the house trying to grab everything he could because he knew that the game he was playing was about to come to an end if he didn't get out of there. With his mother gone and the only living paramedic having escaped, Jimmy was in a rage. He knocked over tables, chairs, lamps, and books from their makeshift bookshelf to recover money and other things of value so he could leave the house.

After he grabbed whatever he could find, he threw everything in a pillowcase and held it tightly in his right hand. With the other hand he grabbed ahold of the wheelchair I was strapped in and tried to push it but it wouldn't budge. So, he grabbed the other handle with his other hand and began to push me to the back door of the house.

Getting me out of the house and to his taxicab was a hard task, but he managed to do it. He opened the trunk of the cab and before he dumped me inside, he untied the straps that restrained my arms to the chair but he left duck tape tied around my wrists. And after he cut the restraints that prevented me from moving my legs, he left the duck tape around my ankles. All he wanted to do was release me from the wheelchair. That was it. I was still bound by his fucking duck tape. I flailed and kicked and tried to scream, but my efforts proved futile.

Once I was inside he slammed the trunk of the car. I wasn't able to do anything. Trying to escape was out of the question. This fool was on a mission and I was caught in the middle. "Mama, I'm coming to get you. I won't let any of those motherfuckers hurt you mama!" I heard him yelling like a maniac.

I felt all the movement when he backed the cab out of the driveway. He stopped on brakes very suddenly and then he pressed down hard on the accelerator and sped off. I had no idea where we were going, but I knew it would be a matter of time before I did.

From a distance I heard sirens. With the screaming and yelling Jimmy was doing the sounds would fade in and out. Even though it was pitch dark in the trunk of the car I still closed my eyes and began a silent prayer.

I know I haven't been the best person in the world but Lord I don't deserve to die. So, please save me. And I promise I'll be the person you want me to be.

While I was praying, I still had this gut feeling that God wouldn't hear my prayer. I mean, come on. I really hadn't been a good person. I've got a lot of people's blood on my hands, starting from my ex-best friend who fucked my man. And then there's Duke, who was the nigga who fucked my best friend and had her turn against me. Next in line was Duke's flunkies, their baby mamas, and the innocent neighbor who was at the wrong place at the wrong time. But let's not forget Katrina, who was married to my former boss Neeko, but had a love child by Duke and no one knew about it. I used to hate her ass in the beginning. But after she helped me get out of her house the night Duke and his boys tried to kill me was a debt that I'd never be able to pay.

In my travels, I learned to love and hate niggas. My life has been one big fucking mess! It seems like bad shit always follows me. I've never asked a nigga for shit. I've always worked hard for my stuff. And the motherfuckers I did rob only got payback because they hurt me. From when I was a little girl I wanted the fairytale life all those other bitches got. I was pretty with a banging ass body. So, why was I always getting shortchanged? What was wrong with me?

While I talked to God, I noticed that my voyage with Jimmy was getting rockier and the car kept swerving from side to side. And when the sirens came within a short distance of the cab and Jimmy continued to shout more obscenities, I knew we were on a high-speed chase. "Y'all motherfuckers ain't gonna get me alive!" I heard him yell. And then I started hearing gunshots. Bang! Bang! Bang! That's when I knew that Jimmy was shooting at the fucking police. Was this motherfucker trying to kill me and him? "Hey, somebody's back here." I screamed through the gag even though I knew I wouldn't be heard. I turned my body around in a way so that I could kick the door of the trunk. My main objective was to try to kick it open. "Somebody's in the trunk." I screamed while I kicked the trunk. One part of me knew that what I was doing wasn't going to help my situation. It did however give me a feeling of hope that someone would hear me.

Bang! Bang! Bang! Jimmy fired three more shots at the police. This time the police returned gunshots.

Boom! Boom! Boom! Boom! Boom! The gunshots that were fired by the police had more force. In fact, one of the shots penetrated the door of the trunk. The shot missed me by less than an inch. I started going crazy. "Please! Please! Somebody is back here! I don't want to die!" I cried.

Jimmy kept the gunfire going. Bang! Bang! Bang! "Y'all think y'all better than me? I'm God! Y'all can't touch me. I'm invincible!" He yelled.

Once again the cops returned gunfire. Boom! Boom! Boom! This time the bullets penetrated another part of the car because before I knew it the car felt like it was in the air. I couldn't feel the gravel underneath the tires. And then the car started turning over and over. My body tossed and turned at least four or five times and then the car collided into something hard. BOOM! My neck jerked and I heard a cracking noise. I couldn't move because my body was twisted around and I had all my weight weighing down on my head and neck. I couldn't move an inch. I tried to figure out how to get out of this position but I couldn't because my wrists were still tied together. And then out of the corner of my eye I saw flames. "Oh my God! Somebody help me! This car is on fire." I tried to scream but I was still wearing this fucking gag.

I started praying again. *God please help me. I don't want to burn up in this car. I will do anything Lord. Please God help me! I can't leave this earth like this.*

Even though my prayer was sincere I knew I was about to die. So, as the smoke became thicker and the flames got more intense, I started coughing uncontrollably. There was no escaping this time. That's when I stopped fighting it and closed my eyes.

Time to go and meet my maker.

Chapter Nineteen

A Major Fucking Screw Up!

Time was rolling by so freaking slow it was becoming unbearable. Normally when I did undercover stings and stakeouts, I never got this fucking bored. I had only been out here for a couple of hours to say the least. So why was I so out of it?

I turned on some music to get me by, but that did not work either. Listening to Big Sean and Drake only made me think back on my college days and all the dumb ass chicks I used to fuck with. If I had not become an agent, I would have become a Navy Seal. What a life that would have been!

While I bumped my head to Big Sean's song Marvin Gaye & Chardonnay, my cell phone rang. "Agent Foster," I said.

"Hi there Agent Foster," the unfamiliar voice said, "this is Lieutenant Daniels from the Norfolk City Police Department.

"How are you?"

"I'm good sir. I'm calling you because I have some very bad news for you."

"What's the matter?" I asked. My heart dropped into the pit of my stomach. I knew he had to be calling me about Lynise. I mean, what else could he be calling me for?

"Is this about my witness Lynise?" I asked. My heart rate picked up speed.

"Yes, as a matter of fact it is." The gentleman said.

"Where is she? Is she alright?" I wanted to know. This guy wasn't giving me enough information. I needed answers.

"Would it be possible for you to meet me?" he asked me.

"Yes. Of course I can. When?" I questioned him. I was anxious to find out what he knew about Lynise. Was she dead? Was she alive? Whatever it was, I needed to find out. She was my witness and I was responsible for her.

"I'm at the DePaul Hospital on Granby Street."

"What's the address?"

"It's 4987 Granby Street. And I'll meet you inside the Chaplain's Office on the first floor near the Emergency Room entrance."

"Wait, so you're telling me she's dead?"

"Agent Foster, I'm gonna need you to come down to the hospital and we can talk then."

"Okay. I'm on my way." I told him, my heart was doing multiple flips inside my stomach. I hung up with the detective and sped off in the direction of the hospital. I called Agent Humphreys. "Humphreys, I just got a call from Detective Daniels from the Norfolk Police Department and he wants me to meet him at the Chaplains office at DePaul Hospital at 4987 Granby Street. So, I'm gonna need you to be there too."

"Wait a minute, she's dead?" Humphreys wanted to know.

"He wouldn't tell me. So, I'm on my way there now."

"What do you want me to tell Agents Rome and Mann?"

"Don't tell them anything. But I do want you to send them out here to the club to watch Agent Zachary's back. Tell them to leave the house now."

"Copy that."

"Don't forget to keep this mum."

"I got it." Humphreys assured me and then we disconnected our call.

I dodged around every car on the highway to get to the hospital. I needed so desperately to find out what Detective Daniels wanted to tell me about Lynise. I pray that she wasn't dead. But if she was, then I failed at my mission to protect her. News like that would damage me forever. I'm speaking of my career as law enforcement as well as emotionally. Lynise held a special place in my heart. It feels like I may be in love.

Upon entering the emergency room my armpits and the collar of my shirt was completely drenched in sweat. The combination of anxiety and fear gripped me like a glove. I was a nervous fucking wreck!

I approached two elderly women behind the information desk. "Excuse me ladies, can you tell me where I can find the Chaplain's office?"

"Go down this hallway and make the first left turn. The Chaplain's office is the second door on the right." The woman on the right said.

"Thank you so much." I told him both and walked off.

Right before I made the first left turn, my cell phone rang. I stopped in my tracks when I noticed it was Agent Zachary's cell phone number. "Hey Zachary, what's up?" I asked trying not to sound overwhelmed.

"I think I've got a problem." She started off.

"What do you mean you have a problem? What's wrong?" I asked. I was literally taken aback, so I had to switch gears. Even though I was at the hospital en route to the Chaplain's office to find out the fate of Lynise, I had to take a step back and find out what was going on with Agent Zachary.

"Both of the Carter brothers are here at the club right now. And the one named Terrence just approached me and asked me if I was the woman he saw the other day driving down his street?"

"What did you say?"

"I denied it. But he didn't believe me because after I brushed him off he walked out of the club and then he came right back in a couple of minutes later. After he walked back into the club, he looked at me and mumbled something to Malik. I'm thinking he went outside, saw the rental car I was driving and told Malik that I lied to him."

"Damn! Why did this shit have to happen after I left?"

"What do you mean left? You're not outside?" She panicked.

"No. I just got a call from a detective at the Norfolk City Police Department saying he had some information about Lynise, and that I needed to meet him at the Chaplain's office on the first floor of DePaul Hospital on Granby Avenue."

"Are you fucking kidding me? Why didn't you call me and tell me this? Do you realize the danger you put me in?" she spat. I could tell that she was both angry and afraid. But did she realize that I said I had to meet the detective inside the Chaplain's office? I couldn't believe how coldhearted she was being.

"Look, you're gonna be fine. I just got off the phone with Agent Humphreys. I told him to have Agents Rome and Mann get to the club. So, they're en route to you right now."

"That's not good enough. You know I am not supposed to be left alone. We agreed that someone was supposed to have my back every minute I am here."

"I know. I'm sorry I dropped the ball." I let out a long sigh. "It's just that I got caught up by the detective's call.

"I understand all of that, but do you see what kind of position you put me in?"

"Listen Agent Zachary, I'm sorry. Now let's move past this. I told you Agent Rome and Agent Mann are on their way to you as we speak. So what I want you to do is get the hell out of there." I warned her. She was around some very deadly men and I feared for her life.

"Okay, let me get the keys for the rental car and then I'm gonna get out of here."

"Hurry."

"I will."

"Call me when you are on the road."

"Alright,"

Chapter Twenty

NOT GIVING UP

After I disconnected my call with Agent Zachary I shoved my cellphone back into the holster and proceeded towards the Chaplain's office. Once again, my heart started to beat uncontrollably. Then the palms of my hands started to sweat. I needed to get a grip on myself.

I rubbed my hands across the side of my jeans to wipe off the sweat and then I let myself inside the office. There was a desk and an empty chair placed next to the left side of the room and then there was a door to the right that led to another room. "Hello," Is somebody here?" I yelled.

"Yes, who are you looking for?" An elderly white man with a headful of silver hair asked as he peered around the corner.

"Well, my name is Agent Foster and I was told by a detective named Daniels to meet him here."

The elderly man walked from around the corner and greeted me with a handshake. He was fully clothed in priestly garments. "Nice to meet you sir. My name is

Mr. Shultz and I am the Chaplain here at DePaul Hospital." He said.

"Nice to meet you too." I replied. I looked around the small room waiting to see if Detective Daniels was going to pop his head out too.

"It's sad how that serial killer had that poor young lady stuffed in the trunk of that burning car."

My heart crashed and burned when I heard the words burning car. What the hell happened? Was Lynise in fact dead? Oh my God! I don't think I'm going to be able to cope with this.

"Burning car? So, she's dead?" I uttered the words slowly. It seemed like everything around me was going in slow motion.

Before the Chaplain could answer me, I heard the office door open behind me so I turned around to see who it was. The Chaplain smiled. "Here's Detective Daniels now," the Chaplain said.

I completely turned around so I could give this detective my full attention. He was nothing like I imagined. I thought I would be meeting a tall, white stocky guy. But in fact, this guy was the exact opposite. We both extended our hands and shook. "You must be Agent Foster." The detective said. His face was blank and I knew what that meant.

"Yes, I am. And you must be Detective Daniels." I said.

"Let's go in the back and have a seat." Daniels told me.

"Sure." I replied.

I followed the detective and the Chaplain back into a seating area of the Chaplain's office. The Chaplain took a seat behind a desk filled with pictures of himself and other priests and files I assumed were of patients that died in the hospital. This further crushed my hopes of Lynise being alive.

After Detective Daniels and I took a seat in the chairs placed on the opposite side of the Chaplain's desk, I braced myself for the inevitable. "What's this I hear about Lynise being pulled from a burning car? Is she dead or alive? What?" I managed to say, despite the knot I had lodged in my throat. Fuck the preliminaries! Just give me the answers I came here for.

"She's on life support right now." Detective Daniels finally said.

"Why? What happened?" I asked. My heart felt like it was ripped from my chest abruptly.

"Well, this matter is still under investigation. But I can say that Lynise was at the residence of an alleged serial killer when the paramedics were called. One of the two paramedics was shot in the head while the other one fled on foot. The paramedic that got away called us and a high-speed chase started. It lasted for about five minutes and ended when the alleged serial killer lost control of his vehicle and slammed it into a tree. Immediately after the car crashed it caught on fire. She suffered a couple of bumps and bruises. But smoke inhalation is what stopped her breathing. She had no brain waves. So, she was immediately placed on life support and is currently in the Intensive Care Unit."

"Where is this serial killer? And how did she get hooked up with him?"

"We don't know the answer to that yet."

"Where is the serial killer? Is he on life support too?"

"No. He only suffered minor injuries. So, he was placed under arrest immediately after we pulled him out of his cab."

"Wait a minute! This guy was a fucking cab driver?"

"Yep. That's what we were told."

"When did this accident happen?"

"Almost two hours ago."

"How did you know to call me?"

"When the firemen pulled her from the trunk of the cab, she had the straps of her purse holstered around her shoulder. And inside that purse had Detective Rosenberg's business card. So I called Rosenberg and wanted to know his affiliation with her and that's when he ran everything down to me about her being held in witness protection and the meeting you guys had at the precinct when a shootout commenced. At the end of our conversation he gave me your cellphone number and here we are. Oh and speaking of Detective Rosenberg, he plans to speak with you in regards to your witness sometime later."

Instead of commenting, I buried my entire face in the palm of my hands. The news about Lynise being on life support hit me like a ton of bricks. What the fuck was I going to do now? Will she live through this? I swear I can't lose her.

While I was trying to cope with the fact that Lynise was depending on life support to keep her alive, I lifted my head back up. "Where is she? Can I see her now?" I asked. At this point, I needed to lay my eyes on her. Trying to imagine her state of being wasn't cutting it for me.

"Yes, you can see her. So, come with me." Detective Daniels agreed. He stood up from his chair and exited the Chaplain's office. I got up and followed him.

We walked onto the elevator and took it to the fifth floor. After we walked off the elevator we walked down a very long hallway. From there we made a right turn and then we took a sharp left turn. During this five-story hike Detective Daniels gave me the run down on the security he formed for Lynise. It was refreshing to know that he cared about her safety. "I just wanted to make sure that if she recovered, she'd have the proper security to protect her, especially with the bounty I heard she had on her head. I heard she had quite a laundry list of people that wanted her head on a platter." He said, sounding like he wanted me to come back with a rebuttal. But I wasn't doing that. So instead, I took the high road.

"I really appreciate that for her." I told him.

As we approached the ICU, I counted at least seven cops standing around guarding a door that led to the room I assumed Lynise was assigned to. The closer I got to the room, the more anxiety sat in the pit of my stomach. I wanted to turn around and leave, but my heart wouldn't let me. I felt totally responsible for Lynise's situation. I figured that if I hadn't forced her to help me arrest Bishop with the federal case, she wouldn't be in this situation. But no, I wanted to be a bad ass and use my authority to use her as bait. Now look at her. I fucked her life up royally.

"Here we are." Detective Daniels pointed out as we approached the crowed of uniformed police officers.

I walked by the cops and peered into the window of the room they had her in. And there was Lynise lying in the bed with gauzes and bandages taped all over her face while the tubes that were attached to a ventilator were enlarged down her throat. To see her like this was truly unbearable.

"The doctor said that it is his hope that she'll be able to breath on her own so she can return to a normal quality of life."

"Did he say how long he'd keep her on life support?"

"No. As a matter of fact, he didn't. But I'm sure he'll be around very soon to give us all of that information."

"Can we go inside her room?"

"No. Not yet. But, I'm confident that it won't be that much longer before we can."

I let out a loud sigh. "Let's hope so." I commented. I was pretty disappointed when Detective Daniels told me that we couldn't go into the room. Did he know how fucking close this woman was to me? This wasn't a fly by night arrangement Lynise and I had. So, I needed to be next to her now.

I think I stared at Lynise through that glass for about seven minutes straight without blinking an eye. I was hurting inside and I couldn't shake it. All I could think about was how this chapter of her life is going to end.

All I can see are flat lines, right now!

Chapter Twenty-One
CASE CLOSED

The doctor for Lynise finally made himself available for Detective Daniels and I to speak one on one with him. "So doctor what can you tell us?" I spoke first.

The doctor glanced into Lynise's room and then he turned back and faced us. "Well, what I can say is that while she's in that coma we're gonna monitor her very closely. And who knows, she may pull through this."

"What are her chances of surviving?" I wanted to know. I needed a shot of hope from somewhere.

"It's too soon to tell." The doctor told me.

"Well, can you tell me when I'll be able to go into her room?"

"After the nurse on duty checks her vitals then you'll be able to go inside and see her."

"Thank you." I said and shook his hand.

As the doctor was about to leave my cellphone rang. I looked down at the caller ID and saw that it was Agent Humphreys calling me. I excused myself from them and stepped over into a corner so I could get a better reception and hear what he had to say. "Humphreys, where are you?" I asked.

"I'm down on the first floor."

"Okay, well I'm on the fifth floor in the ICU. Get on the elevator near the information desk and I'll meet you when you get off."

"Roger that." He replied.

"Daniels my partner is on his way up so I'm gonna meet him at the elevator."

"Sure no problem. See you when you get back."

On my way to the elevator, my cell phone rang again. This time the call came from Agent Rome. "Hey Rome, have you guys made it to the strip club yet?" I asked, immediately after I put him on speaker.

"Yes, we're here. But we can't find Zachary.

"What do you mean you can't find Zachary? I just got off the phone with her. And I gave her specific instructions for her to get the hell out of that club over an hour ago." I barked. While I was I trying to make sense of what Agent Rome had just told me, I hadn't even realized I was walking around the floor in circles. Then a couple of minutes later, the elevator door opened. Agent Humphreys walked into the hallway.

"I've got Agent Rome on the phone and he's telling me that he and Agent Mann are at the strip club and Agent Zachary is nowhere to be found."

"But how can that be?" Humphreys interjected.

"I asked the same fucking question." I snapped.

"Agent Mann and I just rolled up in the club and she's not here. We even asked one of the other waitresses where she was and she couldn't tell us." Agent Rome explained.

"Did you guys see her rental car outside in the parking lot?" I probed more.

"No. It's gone too."

"Well, have you tried calling her? Because she could be very well on her way back to the safe house." I was very agitated at this point and my tone expressed it.

"Foster, we called her over a dozen times and her phone constantly goes straight to her voicemail.

"This is not good. We've got to find her." I said as I continued to pace the floor.

"What do you want us to do?" Agent Rome asked.

"I want you to find her. And I don't care how you do it."

"Where do you want us to start?"

"Start with the owner because she called me not too long ago saying that the Carter brothers were at the club and that one of them recognized her from the other day when she rode by his house. She seemed pretty spooked when he confronted her so she denied that the woman he saw was her. But according to her, he didn't believe her and starting eyeballing her and she began to worry that he may do something to her."

"Are you and Humphreys going to join in on the search for her?"

"We're investigating a lead so I will be in touch. But if you are able to find her before Humphreys and I call you, please call us at once."

"Will do." Rome said and hung up.

Hearing Agent Rome tell me that he couldn't find Agent Zachary felt like a brick had slammed into my head. I was literally thrown off. First it was Lynise and now it is Zachary. What the fuck was I going to do now?

"Sounds like we're gonna have to take a ride to the strip club." Agent Humphreys said.

"Yeah, it does." I agreed.

"Where is Lynise? And how is she?"

"They have her in ICU which is down the hall. Her face looks pretty banged up. And they have her on life support, so she's not looking too good, at least for right now." I explained.

"What did the doctor say about her?" Humphrey's questions continued.

"He really didn't say anything but that they're gonna continue to monitor her and hope that she comes out of this."

"That's it?!"

"Yep. That's pretty much it." I said nonchalantly.

Chapter Twenty-Two
THE WITNESS

I escorted Agent Humphreys back to ICU where Detective Daniels and the cops were. I introduced Humphreys to Daniels and we sat around in a huddle talking while the nurse in Lynise's room took her vitals. "Have you gotten any more information about the serial killer?" I blurted out.

"What serial killer?" Humphreys interjected.

"The serial killer that kidnapped Lynise."

"Well, this is what we learned. The guys name is Jimmy… He is a cab driver and he works in the Hampton and Newport News area. And according to the cab driver's mother who is in the hospital right now being treated for a fall, her son brought your witness to their house over a week and a half ago. She said that her son brought her there because he wanted to marry her and start a life with her. But when the victim started talking down to him she said he put her in her place."

"What floor is this woman on? I would sure like to speak with her." I told Daniels.

"Let's go." he agreed and led the way.

The mother of the serial killer was lying in her hospital bed like she was in a lot of pain. We caught her screaming obscenities to the nurse while her blood pressure was being taken. "You better hurry up and get this shit off me before I get my son on you." She threatened the woman.

"Mrs. Beckford, I will be done with you in a minute." The nurse assured her.

"You said that shit a minute ago. But you're still not done."

"That's because you keep moving your arm so I'm having to start over."

"Excuses. Excuses. I'm so tired of you fast tail girls walking around here like you're better than everybody else."

"Hi Mrs. Beckford, my name is Detective Daniels and I have two agents with me named Foster and Humphreys."

"So what! What do you want with me?" She cut me off.

"Well, we came in here to talk to you about your son Jimmy and maybe get you to answer some questions."

"I've already talked to another policeman. What else do you want me to say?"

"Well, we want to talk about how your son treated the lady you guys had in your house before the paramedics brought you here."

"Well, if you think I'm going to say that I like her,

you are sadly mistaken."

"What didn't you like about her?"

"She acted like she was better than my boy. And she was very disrespectful. I raised my son on the morals and values that I was raised on. I was taught that you never disrespect your elders. And I was taught that when somebody lets you into their house, you need to be grateful. And she wasn't grateful. All she did was complain about everything. She didn't appreciate anything my son did for her. And I didn't like it."

"Well Mrs. Beckford, did Lynise come to your house voluntarily?"

"According to my son, she did. He said, she flagged him down and got into his cab. And when he asked her where she was going, she told him she wanted to come home with him."

"Are you sure your son told you that?"

"Of course I'm sure. Are you calling me a liar?" She growled. She looked like she would've smacked me if I were a little closer to her.

"No ma'am. I just want the facts. That's it." Detective Daniels said.

"Mrs. Beckford, can you tell me where Lynise got all those bruises on her face?"

"My son did it. And she deserved every bit of it."

"What did he hit her with?" I spoke up. I also had questions I needed answered.

"He hit her with his hands."

"Can you tell me why he beat her like that?"

"Have you been listening to anything I said? I told you she was being very disrespectful to me and to my son and he was not having it. Not in our house."

"Mrs. Beckford, is your son a serial killer?"

"I beg your pardon!" she roared. I believe I went below the belt with that question because the level of her anger went up a couple notches.

"Mrs. Beckford, do you know what a serial killer is?"

"Of course I do. I'm not stupid." She replied sarcastically.

"Well, would you please tell us what a serial killer is?" I probed more. It was obvious that this woman was a sociopath, but hearing things more than once gives you the ability to make a sound decision.

"It's a person who kills people." She answered.

"Mrs. Beckford, is your son Jimmy a serial killer?"

"No. He is not."

"Mrs. Beckford, have you ever seen your son kill someone?"

"No. I haven't."

"Mrs. Beckford, are you lying to me?"

"Who do you think you're talking to young man? Do you know that my son will kill you if he finds out that you disrespected me? We don't stand for that type of mess."

"I'm sorry Mrs. Beckford, we don't want that to happen."

"Well, you better mind your business before I tell

him what you did." She warned me.

"Mrs. Beckford, can you tell us how many women had Jimmy brought back to your home?"

"I can't say. I don't remember." She replied and turned her face towards the wall.

"Do you want to help your son Mrs. Beckford?"

"What kind of stupid question is that? Of course I want to help my Jimmy."

"Well in order to do that, you're gonna have to start by telling us how many women had your son brought home?"

"I don't know. I lost count." She told us.

"Was it more than five?

No. It was more than that."

"Was it more than ten?"

Yeah, I believe so.

"Can you give us any of the names of these women?"

"I can't recall."

"Can you tell us what some of their names start with?"

"I don't remember. Maybe one of their names was Chrissy I think."

"Any other names?"

"I told you I don't remember."

"Will you at least try? You would be bringing closure to a lot of families if you did it." Detective Daniels said.

Mrs. Beckford laid there like she was jogging her

memory. Then after a minute and a half she finally said, "I think I remember a woman named Maggie. That's it."

"Did Jimmy rape any of those women?"

"No, he didn't. At least not around me."

"Thank you Mrs. Beckford," Daniels said.

"Yes. Thank you. We appreciate all your help." I chimed in.

Moments after we exited Mrs. Beckford room, Detective Daniels, and Agent Humphreys, and I stood in a huddle so we could put our heads together. It was do or die at this point.

After having that brief chat with the serial killer's mother, we knew that Lynise had stepped into another world after she got into the taxicab with that psychopath. And to have seen a dozen of news clips on TV about this guy made me even angrier. How could I have let this sneak by me? I sincerely dropped the ball on this one.

"Hey Daniels let me have a few minutes with my partner and we'll meet you back in ICU."

"Okay. No problem. See you guys in a few minutes." He said and walked off.

"That shit that lady said was fucking bizarre. And to thank that Lynise went through all of that shit at the hands of her son is fucking nuts."

"Yeah. That's why I'd give anything to get that motherfucker in a room by himself. I would take his life from him with one fucking blow to the head." I replied, spitting venom from my mouth.

"Calm down Foster. We found Lynise. She's here getting the best medical treatment this place has to offer. So, let's focus our energy into finding Agent Zachary."

"Yeah, you're right. It's just that she's been through a lot of shit. And what woman you know could put up with all the shit she's been through?"

"I can't say."

"Exactly. That's why I need just a couple of minutes with that fucking pervert so I can show him what it feels like to put his fucking hands on a woman." I growled.

"Come on Foster. Let's redirect our energy so we can find out where Zachary is." Humphreys said as he pat me on my back.

Chapter Twenty-Three

DO OR DIE

Humphreys and I went into the lounge area for families. It was empty so we thought this would be perfect so we could talk. "Get Rome on the phone and see if he has any new news." I instructed Agent Humphreys.

I watched Humphreys as he dialed Agents Rome's cellphone number. To our surprise he didn't answer. So Humphreys dialed his number again but there was still no answer. So he called Agent Mann. Agent Mann answered his phone on the third ring. "Hey Mann, what's going on? Where is Rome?" I heard Humphreys ask.

"He's inside the strip club."

"Well, that explains why he's not answering my call. Have you guys been able to locate Agent Zachary?"

"No. We haven't. Rome is in the club talking to a few girls hoping to get a lead from them."

"What are you doing outside the club? Why aren't you in there watching his back?"

"Trust me, he's fine. He doesn't need me."

"Have you guys been able to talk to the strip club

owner?"

"Well, we tried to do that but he had already left the club when we asked for him."

"Are the Carter Brothers there?"

"No. This club is dead. There's only a few street punks inside the club getting lap dances but that's it. If the Carter brothers were here earlier, they're gone now."

Not at all satisfied by the work that Agents Rome and Mann were putting in to find Agent Zachary, I snatched Humphreys cell phone from him. "Hey listen Mann, I'm sending Humphreys out there to help you two find Zachary because what I've heard so far is unacceptable. You guys need to burn that fucking street up out there and find her."

"Foster, we're using all the resources we have."

"That excuse isn't good enough for me. I just talked to her not too long ago so she can't be that far. Now if I wasn't over here at this fucking hospital looking after Lynise, I would be with you guys tearing down every door until I found our fellow agent. For all we know, she could be in fucking danger! And you're telling me you're using what resources you have! Don't ever come at me like that again Mann or I will have your fucking badge." I roared. I felt like a seething predator ready to devour those lazy motherfuckers.

"Alright. We'll handle it until Humphreys gets out here." Mann replied calmly.

Once I said what I had to say, I handed Humphreys his cell phone and walked away.

Humphreys disconnected the call and ran behind me to catch me before I got back on the elevator. "You know you just told Mann that you were here at the hospital, right?"

"Yes, I realized that, but at this point I don't even care. Those guys are fucking lazy! And I can't take it."

"Well, you know that he's going to tell Rome the news?"

"Like I said, at this point I could really care less. I've got too much shit to worry about than to worry about those two jerk offs! They're a big fucking joke. And as soon as we get back to New Jersey, I'm switching their details to another unit."

"You know you're gonna open up a can of worms if you do that?"

"And that's what I want." I replied sarcastically and then I turned away from Humphreys and walked towards the elevator. "Be careful out there. And call me as soon as you get any new developments." I instructed him.

Just like that. I got one elevator going up. And he got on the other elevator going down to the first floor. With Agent Humphreys handling Agent Zachary's detail, I felt like I could concentrate on Lynise and her recovery. It felt like a load was lifted.

On the way up to the fifth floor all I thought about was that Lynise would have a speedy recovery and then we could leave this place. I was taking her back to New Jersey. Better yet, I'd relocate with her. I had to have her in my life. And if that meant that I had to resign, then so be it.

Chapter Twenty-Four

LIFE

We were finally given the green light to go into Lynise's room. Detective Daniels encouraged me to go in the room first out of respect, of course. But immediately after I stepped inside and closed the door, I had this weird feeling come over me. Seeing her lying in that bed like that gave me an eerie feeling. She looked like she was dead. I wanted so badly to get Detective Daniels to accompany me, but I decided against that. I figured I'd look like a fucking wimp asking another man to stand by my side while I visited a woman that I fucked and was chosen to protect. Talk about sheer embarrassment.

I walked up to her bed and looked at her from head to toe. I examined her face and her arms, all while thinking about why that fucking serial killer beat her like this. Lynise was really fucked up. Not only did he alter her facial features, he also caused her to be on life support. I swear I wish I could see that bastard now. I'd kill him on the spot. No questions asked.

After I checked out every inch of her body, I sat in the chair placed next to her bed and wondered if she'd ever come out of this. I also wondered that if she did, would she go back to her old ways? I guessed time would tell.

I sat there and tried to think of the good things that she and I did together. I even thought back to when she and I had our first unofficial date. Those times were good. So, I reasoned to myself that if I could think about the good times Lynise and I had, then God would spare her life and bring her back to me. And I promised that this time I wouldn't ever take my eyes off her.

While I reminisced, I heard two knocks on the door. "Who is it?" I asked.

"Its Detectives Whitfield and Rosenberg. Can we come in?" Rosenberg replied.

"Sure come on in."

Both men entered the room. I noticed that Detective Daniels stayed outside in the hallway.

I stood up to greet them. "How is everything gentlemen?" I said.

"We were hoping you'd tell us." Detective Rosenberg said.

I sat back down in my seat. "Let's just say it's the same shit but on a different day."

"How is she coming alone?" Rosenberg asked.

"Everything's steady. But she'll pull through."

Detectives Rosenberg and Whitfield walked up to Lynise's bed to get a closer look. "Can you tell me why she always gets hooked up with the wrong people?" Rosenberg asked.

Shocked by his comment, I asked him to repeat himself. "What the fuck did you just say?" I barked.

"Look Foster, I didn't come in here to rain on anyone's parade." Rosenberg commented.

"So then what do you call it?" I raised my voice. This guy was treading on thin ice.

Detective Whitfield interjected. "What he's trying to say is that your witness isn't what you think she is."

"Don't you two think that this is not the appropriate time to talk about her character? I mean, geesh…., she is lying here in a fucking coma!" I snapped.

"Sounds like you've gotten a little bit too attached." Detective Rosenberg chimed in. "I mean, isn't that a violation of federal agent's code of conduct?"

I stood back to my feet. "So, just what are you insinuating?" I barked. I was standing on one side of the bed and Rosenberg and Whitfield were standing on the opposite side.

Whitfield looked at me while he placed his arm in front of Rosenberg. "We're not getting anywhere by doing this." He said.

"You need to address that shit to your partner." I roared.

By this time Detective Daniels had stormed into the room. "What's going on guys?" he said.

"Detective Daniels escort these fucking creeps out of here before I call Marshall Law on their ass!" I replied sarcastically.

"Oh so now you're a tough guy?!" Detective Rosenberg challenged me. The motherfucker was trying to test my patience.

Detective Daniels threw up his arms. "Calm down gentlemen! This is not the time nor the place to be doing this."

"Detective Daniels please escort these half ass cops out of here before I get Obama to shut this hospital down." I spat. I was fucking pissed about how these local ass cops were treating me, which is why I threw President Obama's name out there. I have never had a conversation with the president nor had I ever been in his presence. But it felt good to name drop. These guys' faces looked like shit afterwards.

"Alright, detectives let's exit the room." Detective Daniels instructed them.

I smiled. "See you later, gentlemen." I said.

"Oh don't worry, we will see you and your witness as soon as we can prove that she is tied to the murders of her best friend and Duke Carrington." Rosenberg hissed.

"And we'll be waiting," I barked. I wasn't fazed by their idol threats. Those two small time cops had no authority or jurisdiction over Lynise and I will make sure it stays that way.

After those two left the room, Detective Daniels sprung a few questions my way. "I'm sorry that had to happen, right now. But I've got to ask, do you think that there's some validity to those accusations?"

"Detective Daniels I am not naïve. Of course I have some concerns about her involvement in those murders. But I can't entertain that right now because for one, she's lying in this bed fighting for her life. And two, she's my witness for a much bigger case. So, my advice for those play cops that just left the room is, do your job. That's your case. Don't bring that shit to me."

"I can understand where you're coming from with that." He agreed.

"Thank you. I really appreciate that." I told him.

Detective Daniels and I chatted about thirty minutes but then it ended when my cell phone started ringing. I asked him if he'd watch Lynise while I took the call in the hallway. He obliged.

"Hello," I said as I walked into the hallway.

"Hey Foster, we've got a problem." Agent Humphreys said. His voice didn't sound right.

"What's wrong now?" I snapped. It seemed like everything was falling apart all around me.

"I'm over here at the strip club and I don't see anyone. Agent Zachary's rental isn't here nor Agents Rome and Mann."

"Have you tried to call them?"

"Yes I've tried to call them over a dozen times. But they won't pick up."

"Have you asked anyone there had they seen them?" I wanted to know. I mean, it's not like the fucking strip club is three stories tall. You can walk through the entire club and it would only take two minutes to do it.

"Yeah, as a matter of fact, I have. I asked a few of the waitresses had they seen them and they said they saw them talking to the owner Malik about twenty minutes ago. I also asked them when was the last time they saw the new waitress and they said that she left in her car like she was in a rush."

"Damn! This cannot be happening." I said.

"So what do you want me to do now?"

"I want you to keep trying to get Rome and Mann on the phone. Call Agent Zachary's cell phone too. I'm gonna also do it on my end, but if you don't get any leeway then head back over to the hospital."

"Okay." He said. And right when I was getting ready to disconnect our call, Agent Humphreys blurted out, "Hey Foster, I think I just saw Agents Rome and Mann's car."

"Where was it?"

"It just rode by the parking lot of the strip club."

Well go catch them and call me back after you speak with them, because I need to know what the fuck is going on!"

"Will do."

Detective Daniels approached me in the hallway immediately after I got off my call. "Got a moment?" he asked me.

"Yeah, sure. What's up?" I replied.

"I just wanted you to know that I'm about to get out

of here and head back to the office. I've got a few things to do before I head home before the night's over."

"Oh, okay. That's understandable. Take care of your business."

"Is there anything you need before I leave?" Detective Daniels wanted to know.

"No. I'm good. I'm just gonna stick around here for the rest of the night."

"Are your agents gonna come back?"

"Yes, they're on their way back here as we speak." I lied. I couldn't let this man know how fucked up my partners were. Our unit has become so unorganized it was pathetic.

"Okay. Well, I'm gonna have two of my uniformed officers to stick around until your agents get back. Is that alright with you?"

"I'd really appreciate that."

"Okay. Well, it's done. Now if you need anything don't hesitate to call me. I keep my cellphone on all night."

"Sounds great. Thanks detective."

"No problem." He said as we shook hands.

Immediately after we shook hands he left two of his officers' instructions while the other three cops followed him to the elevator. I waved them off and headed back to Lynise's room.

I took a seat back in the chair beside her bed and started massaging her left arm. Her body was warm and it felt good touching her, especially after giving up hope that I'd never see her again. This was a triumphant moment for me. She was now safe and sound. And I vowed that no one else would ever take her from me again.

I'd die first before I let anyone hurt her.

Chapter Twenty-Five
GOING OUT WITH A BANG!

An hour went by and the nurse on duty was back in Lynise's room to check her vital signs again. She must've seen the sadness in my eyes when I looked at Lynise because she spoke about it. "Don't look so sad." She said.

"Is it that noticeable?" I asked her.

"Yes, it is. But I also see how much you lover her too."

I got choked up when she recognized the love I had for Lynise. I really didn't know how to respond to it. So, I said nothing and smiled.

"How long have you two been married?" she continued to question me.

"We're not married." I told her.

She smiled back. "You mean, you're not married yet?"

I smiled once again. "Are you psychic?" I joked. Trying to make light of the situation.

"I've had people ask me that." She cracked another smile.

"Well, all I can say is you're good." I replied and looked back down at Lynise. "Do you think she'll come back?"

"I'm not at liberty to say. But I've seen a lot of cases where the patient did come back."

"On the average, how long did it take?"

"Well, it can happen as soon as a few days, and then I've seen some cases where it took months. It just all depends on the patient."

"What would make her chances good?"

"That's kind of hard to say. There is really nothing that anyone can do at this point. Just sit there and continue to talk to her. Who knows, she may be able to hear you."

"Thank you. I really appreciate what you're doing for her."

"No problem. That's what I am here for."

While the nurse continued to work on Lynise, my cellphone rang again. I looked down at the caller ID screen and saw Agent Humphrey's number come up on the screen. I knew I couldn't take the call in the room so I got up to leave. "Will you please excuse me for a moment?" I told her.

"Sure." she replied.

When I got back into the hallway I walked by the two police officers standing outside the door and headed to the other end of the hall. I needed as much privacy as I could get. "Humphreys, got some news for me?" I asked the second I pressed down on the send button and placed the phone up to my ear.

"We got a problem." Humphreys said.

"I'm so sick of hearing about all these fucking problems we have. When are we going to fix something? And where the hell is Agents Rome and Mann? Did you catch up with them?" I growled. I was over all of this bullshit!

"No. That car I saw wasn't theirs."

"Have you found out where Agent Zachary was?"

"That's what I wanted to talk to you about."

"Well, talk."

"I can't. Not over the phone. It's too risky."

"Well, then how do you want to talk about it?"

"I'm about three minutes away from the hospital now. So, meet me outside in the parking lot of the emergency room."

"Okay. I'm on my way down there now."

"Alright."

Out of common courtesy I told the cops that I was going out of the hospital for a couple of minutes and that I needed them to keep a watchful eye out for Lynise while I was gone. They assured me that they'd take care of her. So, I raced down to the first floor.

A gust of wind hit me after I exited the hospital. And for the first time I can honestly say that I loved it. It was a breath of fresh air. And then I started thinking about how we take shit like this for granted. I can say that this brief experience definitely made me appreciate the little things.

While I admired the solace of nature, I quickly snapped back into reality when I noticed Agent Humphrey's car drive up. As he parked his car, I started walking in his direction. By the time I got within arms distance of the car the driver's side door opened. "I can't wait to hear this bullshit you're about to lay on me." I said.

"Oh, I doubt that very seriously." An unfamiliar voice said and then out popped the head of the strip club owner Malik. A second and a half later the back door window rolled down, but I couldn't see a thing until the barrel of a pistol reared its ugly head with a silencer attached. I didn't know whether to pull out my pistol or run for my life.

"What can I do for you gentlemen?" I asked. I was nervous as hell. But I kept my cool.

"You thought you'd never see my face again, huh?"

"I actually never thought about it."

"Well, can you tell me why you lied to me about being a cop?"

"I'm not a cop."

"Oh, nigga don't play games with me. If you walk around with a pistol and a badge then you're a cop."

"Well, I can't argue with you on that point." I said, trying to act as calmly as I possibly could. I couldn't see who was in the backseat pointing that gun at me, but I knew I would find out sooner than later.

"So we heard that our girl Lynise is upstairs laying in one of those hospital beds. Now do you want to confirm that for us?" Malik asked.

"Yeah, she's up there, but she was just transferred down to the morgue." I lied.

"That's bullshit and you know it!" Malik snapped.

"No. I'm serious. She just died a little under an hour ago."

"What floor is she on?"

"Listen, I don't know what floor she's on.......," I said, but then I was cut off in mid sentence when Malik yelled at me. " Shut up!" He said and then he said, "let's see if this will change your mind. Let him out of the car."

Before I could blink an eye, Agent Humphreys stepped out of the back seat with a gun pointed at his head. It was the same gun that had the silencer screwed onto the barrel. Holding the gun to his head was Terrence Carter. He was the same guy that questioned Agent Zachary after she passed his home. So I knew this wasn't good.

"Hey listen you guys, if we can put down the guns, I'm sure we can handle this situation in a manner that would benefit us all."

"The only thing that would benefit me is for me to get my hands on your witness." TC commented.

"Wait, how did you know that Lynise was my witness?" I wanted to know.

"The female cop you sent in to spy on my cousin Malik told us everything."

"Where is she?"

"Oh don't worry about her. She's sound asleep."

"What did you do to her?"

"I didn't do anything. You did it when you sent her in and left her all alone."

"That's bullshit! Tell me what did you do to her?"

"It's too late for her. Let's focus on this gentleman right here." He said as he turned his attention back on Agent Humphreys.

I looked in Humphreys eyes and I could tell that he was sorry that he brought these guys here. So, I had to let him know that it was okay. "Hey buddy, it's alright." I spoke up.

"Oh no. It's not alright until I say it's alright." TC roared. "Now tell me where Lynise is before I blow his fucking head off!" he hissed, I knew his patience was about to run out.

"Foster he already knows where she is. He just wanted you away from her room. He's got four guys in there right now looking for her so they can kill her!" Agent Humphreys yelled. And before I could open my mouth, TC fired the gun twice at Humphreys' head. Humphreys' eyes rolled to the back of his head and his body went limp. TC released his grip on Humphreys and he fell to the ground. Life was sucked out of me seeing my partner fall dead right before my eyes. First they killed Agent Zachary, now Agent Humphreys. I had to stop them once and for all.

I grabbed my pistol from my side and ducked down on the ground. I had to take cover to prevent myself from being shot, and then I let off three shots. BOOM! BOOM! BOOM! In the distance I heard shots being fired at me too. They were trying their best to keep me out here. But I couldn't let that happen. I had to get out of here. Lynise needed me.

After firing four more shots I managed to run and ducked behind a few cars before I was able to enter the hospital through another entry. "He's getting away." I heard Malik scream.

As soon as I got into the hospital, I ran into a janitor and asked him to call the police. "Tell them to get to ICU now. They're at least four to five guys up there right now trying to kill the patient on life-support in room 5-Q." I said, panting. I was literally out of breath. But that didn't stop me from getting the word out because I had no one left to back me. Agent Zachary and Agent Humphreys were dead. And Agents Rome and Mann were nowhere to be found.

Instead of taking the elevator, I ran up all five flights of steps. And when I reached the fifth floor, I reloaded my ammo. I opened the door to the fifth floor stairwell and peered into the hallway. At that moment, I heard a whole bunch of screaming and gunshots being fired so I had no idea what I was up against. I was sure that TC and Malik had already warned his boys that I was on my way back to the room so I also knew that I had to be very precise when I make my move.

My heart started beating rapidly after I entered into the hallway. With every turn I made, I planted myself against the wall before I made my next move. "Come on Foster, you gotta save her." I said in a whisper like tone. I counted to the number three and then I moved down to the next corner. Then I peeped around the corner. "Fuck!" I hissed. My heart rate tripled in speed when I saw all of the hospital staff lying in their own pool of blood. I knew that there was no way I was going to see Lynise alive after this.

Still panting I very carefully moved down the hallway with the hopes that I wouldn't be seen. "Check every room until you find her?" I heard a voice that sounded like TC. So I moved closer to where his voice was coming from. I held my finger on the trigger, waiting to fire it. I had to step over six bodies before I was able to put a face with the voice. And just like I had suspected, TC and Malik, along with four more men were ransacking this entire fifth floor.

"Put your hands up." I heard about five men say in unison.

I looked to the right of me and saw at least ten policemen with riot gear, pointing their pistols at TC and his boys. But TC and his boys weren't going down without a fight. They raised their guns and started a shootout with all ten cops. BANG! BANG! BANG!

BOOM! BOOM! BOOM! BOOM! BOOM! POP! POP! POP!

BANG! BANG! BANG! BANG! POP! POP! POP!

It was sheer pandemonium on this floor. They put a couple of bullets inside of Malik and two of the guys with him and it was lights out for them. From the looks of it, the cops were handling they're own so I decided to go and find Lynise.

I crawled down on my knees to get out of harms way until I was completely out of sight. I got up on my feet and walked quietly in the direction of Lynise's room. I moved carefully as I made a move on to the next hallway, which was where her room was. After I stopped and peered around the corner and saw that the coast was clear, I moved up quickly. I didn't see the two police officers that were supposed to be guarding her. The hallway was completely deserted. Realizing this made my heart fall to the pit of my stomach. I didn't know whether this was a good sign or a bad one. I held my breath as I crawled over to her room. And when I stood to my feet to look inside the room, I saw that Lynise was lying there unharmed. I rushed into the room and when I tried to lock the door TC stood there before me and let off the first shot through the window. The window shattered and I dove to the floor. "Yeah, you took me right to her! You dumb ass cop!" TC roared as he kicked in the door of Lynise's room.

"My brother is going to be very pleased when he finds out that I finally found the bitch that ruined our multi-million dollar adoption enterprise." TC growled as he aimed the gun at Lynise.

I jumped up from the floor and dove onto Lynise's bed as TC fired one shot after the next. I felt every bullet that went through me. But that didn't matter to me.

Lynise was my main concern. So if it meant that I had to die for her then so be it.

"Put your weapon down!" I heard a cop yell.

I knew he was talking to TC but I couldn't turn my head to see. I was weak and I felt the movement in my body slowly deteriorating. Within the next few seconds I heard another ten shots fired. "He's down." I heard one of the cops say. While that was good for me to hear, I knew that wasn't enough to keep me alive. TC had already shot me four times. It felt like he hit some very important organs, because my blood was leaking from me like a faucet. I searched Lynise's face closely to see if she was still breathing and when I heard the sounds of the life support monitor, my notion was confirmed. So, all I could do at this point was lay my head down on her chest. Leaving this world lying next to her was all I needed. I looked at Lynise for the final time and then I closed my eyes.

Hopefully I'll see her on the other side!

Sneak Peek into:

ERICKA KANE PT. #1

Prologue

My naked body shivered as my blood ran down my face, chest, and stomach. I couldn't stop my legs from shaking. Not to mention, my bladder felt like it would explode at any moment. Wherever they had me, it was literally freezing cold like I was naked in Alaska.

"Hit her again," a man's voice boomed. I braced myself because I knew exactly what was coming next. "Please," I whispered, but my words were ignored. It was clear that these were some very dangerous people and they were not going to have any mercy on me. It also became clear that if I ever got out of here alive, I would go on a serious mission to hunt down each and every one of these motherfuckers and torture them ten times worse than they did to me.

"Agggh!" I let out another scream as I felt the shock waves from the oversized stun gun that was being used to torture me. It had to be something they use on large farm animals to make them submissive. I didn't know how many more high-powered surges of electricity my body would be able to take.

My face was scrunched up and my eyes rolled into the back of my head. Sweat was pouring from every pore on my body. I gagged but nothing came up from my stomach. I was in so much pain I felt like even the organs inside of my body hurt. My heart pounded painfully against my weakened chest bone and my stomach literally churned. I was wishing for death because even that had to be better than what I was feeling at the moment. Another hit with the electric current caused piss to spill from my bladder and splash on the feet of one of my tormentors.

"This bitch pissed on me!" he growled. Then he took his huge hand and slapped me across the face so hard spit shot out of my mouth.

"Daddy! Help me!" I struggled to get the words out as my body jerked fiercely from another hit from the stun gun.

"Please let her go," my father mumbled, his words coming out labored and almost breathless. "Just take me, but let her go," he whispered through his battered lips. I had heard him coughing and wheezing as our captors beat him unmercifully. It was almost unreal what we were going through. As hard as the torture was, it was even harder to see my father in a position of total helplessness. He had always been my hero all of my life. When my mother decided that she didn't want to be a mother anymore, it had been my father who'd made all of the sacrifices to take care of me alone. He was always so strong and heroic to me, but now, he was just as weak and useless as me.

"Daddy," I panted, my head hanging. "Don't let them kill me."

I squinted through my battered eyes and tried to see him, but the bright lights my torturers were using prevented me from catching a real good glimpse of my father. I figured that I would probably never see him again. I could hear the voices around me clearly though, so I knew we were all in close proximity.

"You betrayed us, Eric. You and your little bitch daughter thought you could outsmart us. I should have never trusted you as a business partner. I should have known that such a weak man, who would run from his native country, would give in to these American ideals. You were once a son of Nigeria…a man who loved his country, now a traitor, a betrayer, and a weak ass man. You got too big for yourself. I knew when you came to this country you would think you were the boss of everything. I let you have a good life here. Yes, you were living in a big mansion, rubbing elbows with the wealthy white Americans that you wished you could call your brothers, and most of all working with the police to bite the hand that feeds you," a tall, ugly man with black skin and yellow eyes hissed as he came into focus in my vision. He had stepped around the bright light and I could see every feature of his hideous face. He resembled a Gorilla because there was something grotesque about his features. His nostrils were almost non-existent and those little beady eyes didn't look like they belonged on a human face at all.

"No. I did everything you asked, Kesso. I was always loyal to you and my entire country and my fellow Nigerians. I helped all of the people you sent to me. I gave them jobs. I gave them money. I gave them places to stay. I repaid my debts to you over and over again. I entered into this business unwillingly, but I did it to repay the debts I owed you for helping me get to America. I turned over everything you asked for…including all of the slaves you wanted. All of the money you wanted, even my wife. You even took the only woman that I ever truly loved from me. What more could I do, Kesso? Now, you have my daughter," my father cried as another round of punches landed in his midsection. More cracks and coughs came as the men pounded on my father, breaking bones and injuring his insides. I heard my father's words, but I couldn't believe my ears. Did my mother run to my father's business partner? Did my father get into something that he would never be able to get out of? It was a lot to handle because I had always worshipped the ground that my father walked upon. My heart was breaking watching him suffer. It was worse than any pain my torturers could impose on me right then.

"Daddy! Stop hurting my Daddy!" It was killing me to know he was in all of that pain. After I discovered what my father was into I was devastated, but that didn't change the fact that I loved him and that he was all that I had in the world. I recognized that the position we were in right at that moment was my fault too. My father had pleaded with me to leave the situation alone. He had asked me to stop investigating and to stop trying to dig up the truth. My father had actually pleaded with me to just accept everything the way it was, but I couldn't do it. He knew how stubborn I could be, but there was nothing much he could do about it. I had to keep investigating for myself. I had to call in the assistance of the police. I wanted justice! That was the stubbornness in me that I had gotten from my mother. She was the type of bitch that never backed down from something that she wanted. As much as I hated her, I was like her in a lot of ways…all of her bad ways. Now, my father and I were facing death with no clear way out of the situation. All because of me! If anyone deserved to die, it was me.

"Daddy I'm so sorry! I just wanted to help. I just wanted to make things better. I just needed some answers. I never meant to have this happen to you. I told you Kesso! Just kill me and let my father go! It is me that you want! I was the one who brought all of the heat to your door and pulled the lid off of your business! It was all me…not my father!" I cried some more. I bet this so-called African prince wasn't used to a woman speaking to him like that. I hated him and I didn't care about any traditions.

"Shut her up! I'm tired of her fucking mouth. This little bitch cost me millions of dollars because she wanted to play Nancy Drew…now I want to see her suffer. She's a piece of shit just like her father. She is not worth sharing the same air with," Kesso, the ugly man barked, waving his hands. His goons immediately surrounded me. My heart rattled in my chest, but there was nothing else they could do to me that would hurt me more than the possibility of my father dying at my hands. I gave up at that moment. Whatever was going to happen must've been our fate from the beginning, I reasoned with myself. I kept screaming things that I knew were disrespectful in the eyes of my father's Nigerian counterparts. I wasn't going to be one of those passive women. No! I knew what those bastards were doing to women and I could only hope that the call I had made before they snatched me would help me in the end.

After a few minutes, one of those huge, wrestler type dudes grabbed me by my hair and dragged me across the gravel floor. "Agh!" I screamed. It was like nothing I had ever felt before. I don't know how I didn't slip into shock after all of those hours of torture I had endured. My entire body felt like someone had doused me with gasoline and lit me on fire. I could feel the once perfect skin on my legs and ass shedding away against the rough floor. I didn't want to die, but if I was going to die, I was going to go out fighting. I tucked my bottom lip under my top teeth and gritted.

"Get off of me! Get the fuck off of me!" I screeched so loud that my throat itched. "Fuck all of you! You're all going to burn in hell for what you're doing!" I continued; feeling blood rushing to places on my body that I didn't know even existed. I bucked my body wildly, but all of my fighting efforts were to no avail. Of course they were stronger than me, which meant that I wasn't going to be able to break free. I never dreamed of going out of this life fighting tooth and nail. My father always called me his little African lion and I planned to live up to that name before I died. The man dragging me finally let go of the fist full of my hair he had been holding. He released me with so much force that my head slammed to the floor. I felt something at the base of my skull come loose. I was dazed for a few seconds, but not for long. I was brought back to reality when I felt a boot slam into my ribs. The force was so great that a mouthful of blood spurted from my mouth.

"You don't have such a big mouth now, huh?" the goon hissed, his accent thick and barely understandable.

"Please don't hurt her anymore. I will give you everything I have if you just let her go," I heard my father gurgle.

"It is too late for that. You and your little troublemaker should've thought about that before both of you betrayed me. Now, someone has to pay with their life. There will be no more talking," Kesso said with finality.

The next thing I heard was the ear-shattering explosion of a gun.

"No!!!!!" I belted out, right before my entire world fell apart. Blackness engulfed me and I wondered how it had all come to this. Not even a month ago, my father and I had been so happy.

NEVER TRUST A BITCH WITH POWER

ERICKA

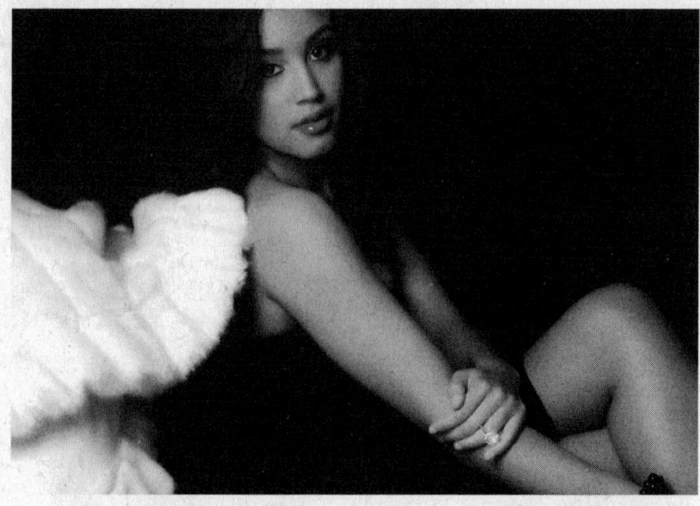

KANE

KIKI SWINSON

NATIONAL BESTSELLING AUTHOR OF WIFEY

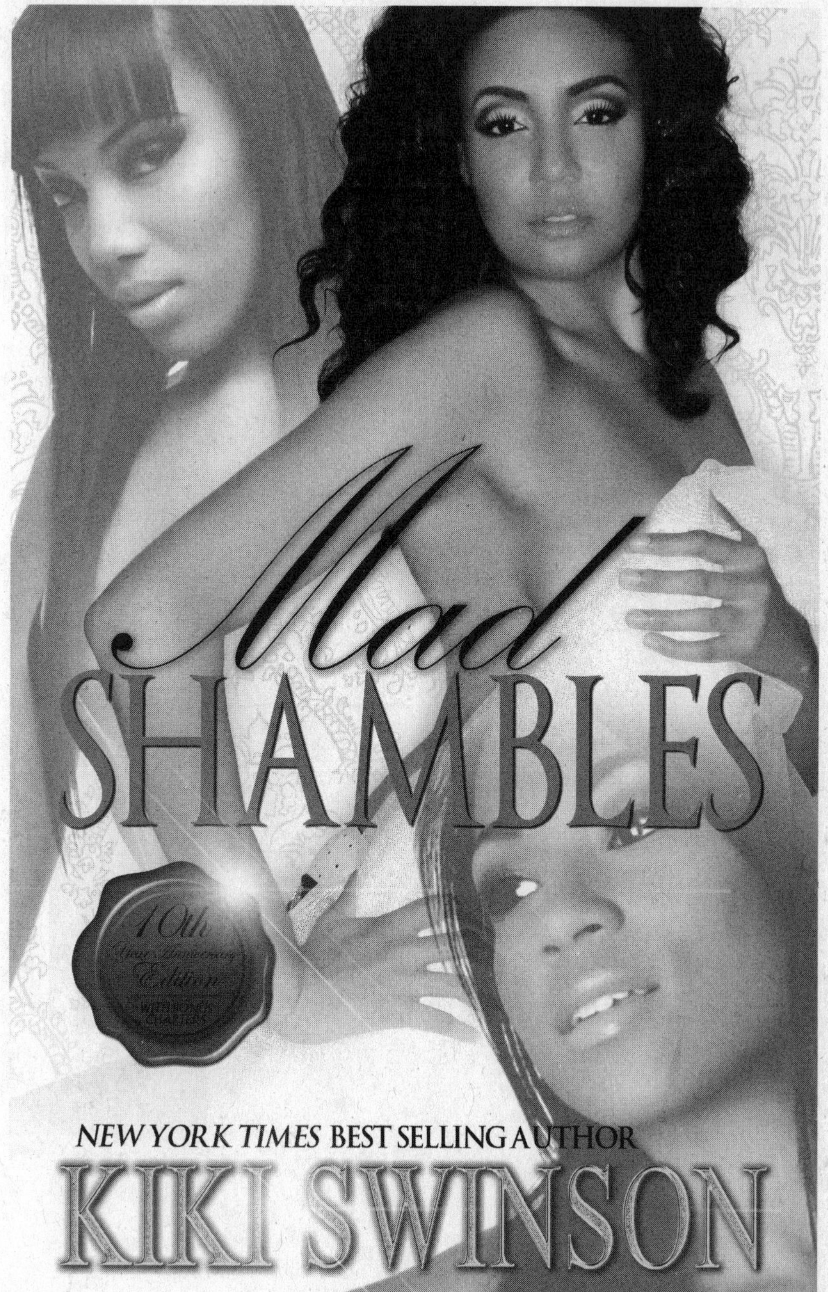
Mad
SHAMBLES
10th Year Anniversary Edition
WITH BONUS CHAPTERS
NEW YORK TIMES BEST SELLING AUTHOR
KIKI SWINSON

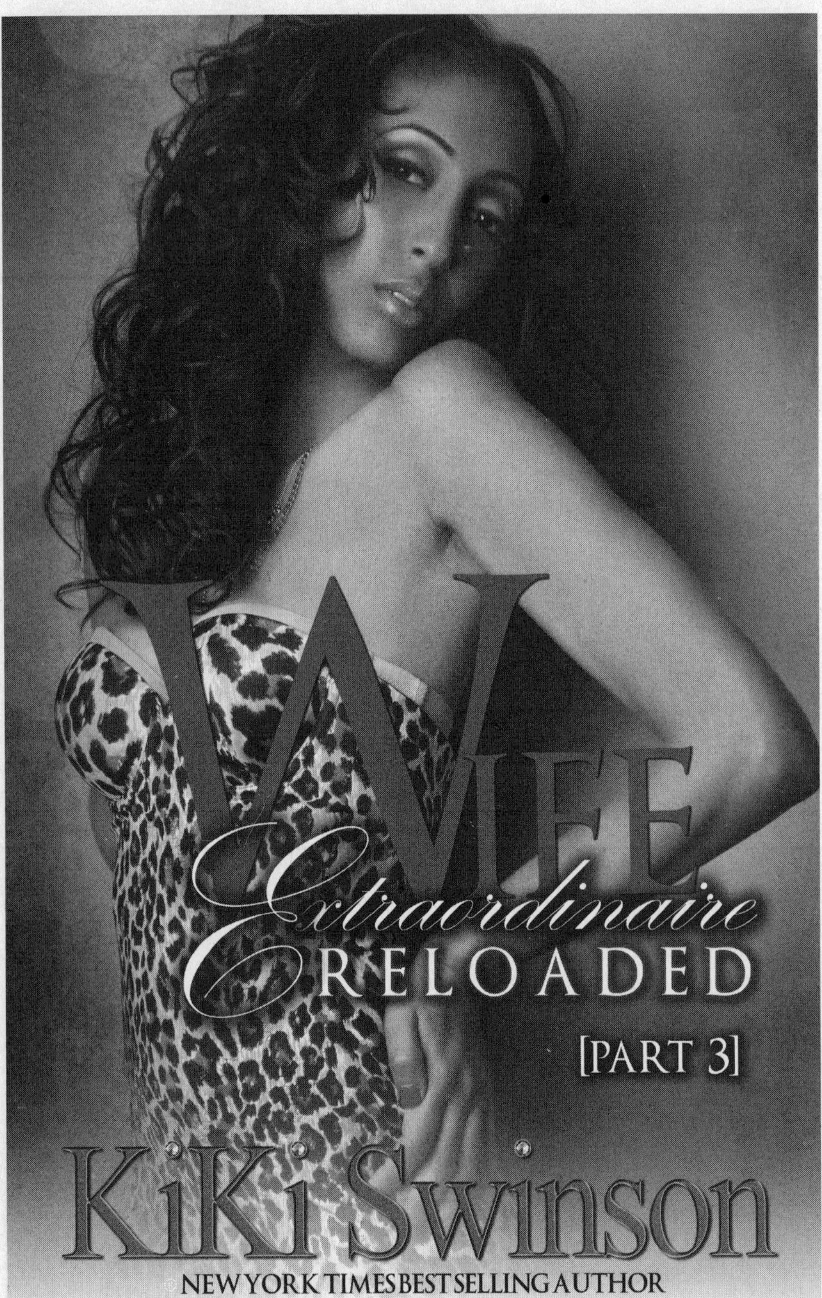
WIFE
Extraordinaire
RELOADED
[PART 3]
KiKi Swinson
NEW YORK TIMES BEST SELLING AUTHOR